THREE FRENCH HENS

Twelve Days of Christmas

Emily E K Murdoch

ARE YOU SIGNED UP FOR DRAGONBLADE'S BLOG?

You'll get the latest news and information on exclusive giveaways, exclusive excerpts, coming releases, sales, free books, cover reveals and more.

Check out our complete list of authors, too!

No spam, no junk. That's a promise!

Sign Up Here

www.dragonbladepublishing.com

Dearest Reader;

Thank you for your support of a small press. At Dragonblade Publishing, we strive to bring you the highest quality Historical Romance from some of the best authors in the business. Without your support, there is no 'us', so we sincerely hope you adore these stories and find some new favorite authors along the way.

Happy Reading!

CEO, Dragonblade Publishing

Additional Dragonblade books by Author Emily E K Murdoch

Twelve Days of Christmas
Twelve Drummers Drumming
Eleven Pipers Piping
Ten Lords a Leaping
Nine Ladies Dancing
Eight Maids a Milking
Seven Swans a Swimming
Six Geese a Laying
Five Gold Rings
Four Calling Birds
Three French Hens
Two Turtle Doves
A Partridge in a Pear Tree

The De Petras Saga
The Misplaced Husband (Book 1)
The Impoverished Dowry (Book 2)
The Contrary Debutante (Book 3)
The Determined Mistress (Book 4)
The Convenient Engagement (Book 5)

The Governess Bureau Series
A Governess of Great Talents (Book 1)
A Governess of Discretion (Book 2)
A Governess of Many Languages (Book 3)
A Governess of Prodigious Skill (Book 4)
A Governess of Unusual Experience (Book 5)
A Governess of Wise Years (Book 6)
A Governess of No Fear (Novella)

Never The Bride Series

Always the Bridesmaid (Book 1)
Always the Chaperone (Book 2)
Always the Courtesan (Book 3)
Always the Best Friend (Book 4)
Always the Wallflower (Book 5)
Always the Bluestocking (Book 6)
Always the Rival (Book 7)
Always the Matchmaker (Book 8)
Always the Widow (Book 9)
Always the Rebel (Book 10)
Always the Mistress (Book 11)
Always the Second Choice (Book 12)
Always the Mistletoe (Novella)
Always the Reverend (Novella)

The Lyon's Den Series
Always the Lyon Tamer

Pirates of Britannia Series
Always the High Seas

De Wolfe Pack: The Series
Whirlwind with a Wolfe

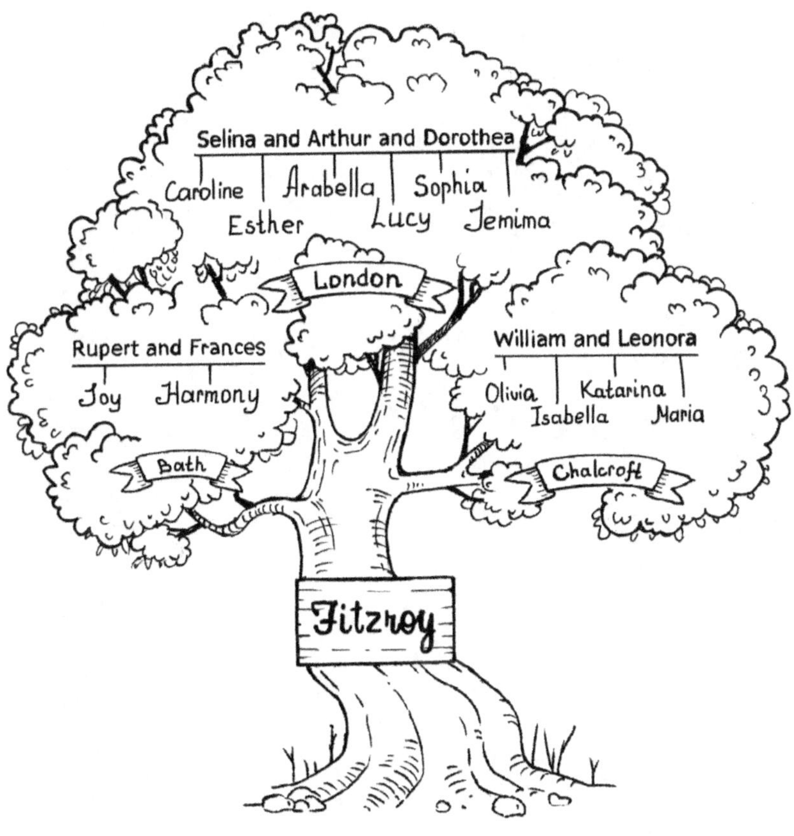

Selina and Arthur and Dorothea
Caroline
Arabella
Sophia
Esther
Lucy
Jemima
London
Rupert and Frances
Joy
Harmony
Bath
William and Leonora
Olivia
Katarina
Isabella
Maria
Chalcroft
Fitzroy

CHAPTER ONE

"Oh, simply charming!"

"I have to admit Almack's has certainly improved this year…"

"—musicians far more impressive than at the latest concert, I must tell you—"

Sophia Fitzroy smiled broadly as she stepped into Almack's, leaving the freezing December chill behind and finding herself enveloped in the warm, almost muggy atmosphere of the absolutely best place to see Society—and be seen.

"Now," said her mother warningly, seeing that smile. "Just because you are out—"

"Doesn't mean I can say what I please," said Sophia with a heavy sigh.

Selina smiled at her daughter. "I could not have said it better myself."

It was on the tip of Sophia's tongue, as she pulled up her long gloves and smoothed down her blue silk gown, that it had been said, repeatedly, but decided against it. This evening was not one to pick a fight with her mother—especially as she had high hopes for her outing this evening.

Almack's.

When one was the youngest of six sisters, one had to become accustomed to being left at home. Why, it was only a year ago that Sophia's parents had deigned to permit her to join Society, a full twelvemonth after her sisters Esther and Lucy had wed.

There was Esther now. Sophia managed not to step on the feet of a footman circulating with a tray of drinks as she crept to the wall, eager to stay out of everyone's way. She did not want any of her sisters to—

Esther waved, beaming as she danced energetically with her husband. Sophia managed a wave but almost knocked a feather out of a woman's elegant hair, and swiftly halted.

The last thing she wished to do was draw attention to herself for all the wrong reasons.

"Now, can you behave yourself?"

Sophia raised an eyebrow at her mother's question. "You have to ask?"

"When you have six daughters, five of whom are married," said her mother dryly, "you will know why I ask. Now, I will only be over there, if you require me to—"

"Go and speak with your friends," said Sophia with a smile. "I know you wish to exchange news of grandchildren. I will be quite safe here—besides, I expect to dance before too long."

Within a moment, she was alone…at least, as alone as anyone could be at Almack's. Though vouchers were rarely given out these days, Sophia was astonished to find a crush in the place, more gentlemen in one room than she had ever seen.

One particularly impertinent one glanced over and grinned, his cravat ridiculously styled and his hair set at a jaunty angle. He elbowed his friend, who turned to display an even more outlandish cravat, who then winked at her.

Sophia flushed and immediately looked at her clasped hands. *Well, the cheek of it!* A gentleman should never even consider such a thing—it was outrageous!

Still…

She glanced up. The two gentlemen were gone.

A strange sort of disappointment settled in Sophia's stomach. It was not as though she wished to be considered a flirt, not when she was the last of her sisters to marry…but still. It would be nice to have a conversation with a gentleman, at least.

Her gaze drifted past the gaggles of mamas exchanging stories of children and grandchildren, crowing over the latest engagement, the gentlemen discussing politics or the latest hunt, and a gaggle of ladies more her age who were laughing heartily.

Sophia's stomach lurched. Her sisters had always been her companions; she had seen no need for friends outside the Fitzroy family…which was all very well. Until they'd married.

There was Arabella, dancing with her husband alongside Esther. Sophia's foot tapped lightly to the beat of the music, a cheerful number that was fast-paced.

Oh, how she longed to dance; to feel the rhythm in her body, the elegant repetition of the steps, the movement with a gentleman…not that she had much practice with the last.

"There you are!"

Sophia smiled as her older sister, Caroline, warmly greeted her. "Here I am."

"And about time, too. I was about to send a servant over to see why Papa was keeping you so long," said Caroline smartly, tapping her sister on the arm. "It was Papa who delayed you, was it not?"

It was impossible not to laugh. "You left home a good while ago, didn't you?"

Caroline frowned. Sophia tried to halt her laughter, but it was rather difficult. The second eldest of the Fitzroys, Caroline had rather scandalized Society by becoming engaged to a simple country doctor…who turned out to be the heir to an earldom.

Now a countess, Caroline had been married near six years, and Sophia could hardly remember what life at home had been like then. Certainly very different to how it was now.

"What difference does that make?" asked Caroline, a haughty sniff in her tone.

Sophia grinned. "It's Mama who takes an age—getting her into that corset!"

"Oh, hush now!" Caroline looked absolutely mortified, glancing around in case they had been overheard.

Which was impossible, as far as Sophia could see. The crush of people in Almack's was only increasing, and the noisy chatter and music lent more privacy.

"You'll have your mouth washed out with soap, if you're not careful!"

Sophia sighed. It was most irritating, being treated as though one was a child, after all this time. Had she not proven herself to be mature enough to be attending balls and card parties?

In short, was she not ready for…*romance?*

She blushed a little merely at the thought. All she wanted was a dance, so she would start with that—but in the crush of the room, there was no opportunity to be introduced to anyone new, and none of their acquaintance could be seen.

"You should be dancing."

Sophia sighed. That was the trouble with Caroline: first to point out problems, rarely offering solutions. "Yes, Caroline, I would like to dance—but as no one has asked me…"

The temptation to suggest to her uptight sister that she could approach a gentleman and ask for his hand for the next dance flitted across Sophia's mind, drawing a smile to her face, but she did not give in.

Caroline would never countenance such a thing…and Sophia was not entirely certain whether she would have the bravery for it.

Her gaze drifted once more over the loud, chattering gentlemen. Tall, short, handsome, uninteresting, loud, quiet…there were so many of them. So many choices.

Though in truth, Sophia reminded herself, *it is the gentlemen in the room who have the choice.* Ladies simply could not go about asking gentlemen to dance!

"I am sure someone will ask you to dance," Caroline said soothingly. "Eventually."

Sophia scowled, but quickly restored her expression to one of benign interest. *Well, it was most provoking!* Here they were, coming up to Christmas with everyone who was anyone in Town…yet this was the second ball in a row in which no one had asked her to dance.

Yet.

"What I really want," she found herself saying wistfully, "is a scandalous romance."

"Sophia Fitzroy!"

Sophia had never seen Caroline look more outraged: eyes wide, mouth open, a splotchy red seeping across her face.

"You cannot possibly mean that," hissed the Countess, glancing around once more to ensure they could not be overheard.

Not that it would matter, Sophia thought with a wicked grin. No one would take her seriously; she was only saying it to wind up her sister. Mostly.

Sophia had attended all five of her sisters' weddings, and each had been remarkably fine affairs. But if she was not much mistaken, a few had welcomed children… Well.

Eight months later.

She had never spoken to them about such things; even between sisters, there were some things one did not ask. But still. She was not a complete fool. Her sisters had…had allowed themselves to be bedded before they were married!

Sophia could not understand precisely how the news had never got out of the family—perhaps it had, but she had never read about it in the scandal sheets.

It was her turn, finally, to have her own wild romantic encounters.

Not that she would permit herself to be bedded before she was married, but Sophia could dream of wild kisses on staircases, embraces in the dark—

"I do not mean anything so…well, *wild* as you are supposing," Sophia said haughtily, much to Caroline's chagrin, "but it would be pleasant to be whisked off one's feet by an elegant gentleman whose only wish is to please me."

To please her.

Perhaps that should not have been her precise wording. Caroline looked to the ceiling as though begging for silent help from the heavens, then looked fiercely at Sophia. "If you cannot speak civilly in such a place as this, I shall have no choice but to send you home!"

"I am not a child, Caroline," Sophia said briskly. Honestly, she was having to say this more and more often these days. "I cannot be sent to bed—I want adventure! I want a scandalous romance, I say, and I do not see why I should have to censor myself to my sister!"

"A scandalous romance?" A deep voice snorted. "You'll be lucky, Miss Fitzroy—sixth to hold that title. You think you deserve to be…what was it, whisked off your feet?"

Sophia's stomach lurched, and her chest was tight. She had not actually thought anyone could hear their conversation…but evidently someone had.

Swallowing hard and telling herself she had not done anything wrong—not materially wrong, anyway—Sophia slowly turned as the dance ended and people applauded politely.

But one man was not. A tall gentleman, with dark hair and blazing green eyes—eyes fixed on her.

A heat Sophia had never known rushed through her body, so quickly she felt her balance tip. Managing to steady herself, she tried to take in the sight of him: stylish yet not lavish coat and waistcoat, a cravat, and an air of arrogance she had never seen before.

The heat that rushed through her body reached her cheeks, and Sophia did her best to hold the stranger's gaze, challenging as that was.

"A scandalous romance? You'll be lucky, Miss Fitzroy…"

How dare he! How dare a gentleman say such things, and in public, too! It was an outrage!

"And you are?" she said rudely, trying to ignore just how handsome he was.

Goodness, anyone else blessed with those cheekbones and those remarkably kissable lips would have stirred her, Sophia was sure—but this heat she felt was rage, not attraction.

As though she would be attracted to a man who spoke to her like that!

"Tired of hearing your nonsense, I must say," said the irritating gentleman with a laugh. "Begging your pardon, your ladyship."

Sophia glanced at Caroline, who was unaccustomed to being spoken to in that way.

"I think my husband calls me," said Caroline vaguely, hastily looking in the other direction. "Coming, dear—do excuse me."

"Caroline!" Sophia said, attempting to grab her sister's hand but having little luck.

Her elder sister stepped away, leaving her to her miserable fate.

The stranger grinned. "Abandoned so quickly?"

"Nothing of the sort," Sophia bit back, hardly knowing why she was indulging such a rude gentleman. She should walk away without a curtsey after such arrogance, such rudeness!

But something she did not precisely understand kept her there. It was probably the crush, Sophia told herself. Yes, it would be rather difficult to extricate herself from this position by the wall, there were so many people around.

Strange. She seemed only aware of one of them.

"I think it rather daring of you to openly criticize a young lady in public," Sophia said brightly, as though she had arguments with strangers all the time. "Particularly the younger sister of the Countess of Cheshire and the Duchess of Kendal."

Instead of being impressed by her sisters' titles, as she had expected, the gentleman merely rolled his eyes.

"Yes, yes, very fine," he said dismissively, "but I would have thought you, Miss Fitzroy, would recognize a title is just an adornment atop a man. The man himself must be impressive, or else the title merely looks ridiculous."

Ridiculous? How dare he suggest—At least, Sophia *thought* he was suggesting her two brothers-in-law were ridiculous. Wasn't he?

"What would you know about titles?" she managed.

The man smiled wickedly. "Oh, I know everything that goes on here. I know all about you."

A flutter in her chest prevented her from speaking for a moment, and a passing gaggle of ladies pushed the gentleman a step closer. They were now but a foot apart. It was most irritating to have him so close. Just when she wanted to escape him, too.

Now he was laughing. "Orlando Dunbar, at your service."

"I do not need servicing from you," Sophia said haughtily. Her cheeks scalded as the words from her mouth repeated in her mind. "I meant—"

"I know precisely what you meant," said Orlando with a grin. "My, my, it appears my information was incorrect."

Information? Trying desperately to keep calm after her rather indelicate turn of phrase, Sophia swallowed. She was not going to continue making a fool of herself before this man. What a shame he was such a cad. If he had been mildly entertaining, she might have asked to be introduced, hoping for a dance.

Now all she could hope was to extricate herself from the conversation.

"Yes, I was informed all the Fitzroy sisters were married, save one, and she was the prettiest one," said Orlando. "That would be you, I take it."

Sophia swallowed. "You are very rude, aren't you?"

"Probably." The incorrigible gentleman shrugged. "But I find the ladies like it. Don't you?"

"I—I don't know what you're…" Sophia's voice faded.

This man, this *Orlando*, was making it difficult to concentrate, which was infuriating. Sophia was never usually one to struggle for words, even if she did not actually say them.

But this gentleman, this cad, this fool…the way he looked at her, as though hungry and uninterested at the same time…it was unaccountably interesting.

Sophia swallowed, then held her head up high. "I do not see any reason why anything should prevent me from—from romance, and dances, and all sorts of things like…like that."

She had never spoken so boldly to a gentleman before. Well, perhaps Percy, but Lucy's husband did not count. They had all known him since they were children.

Orlando raised an eyebrow. "And perhaps it won't, but if you ask me, Miss Fitzroy, you, like all youngest sisters, are more likely to stay a spinster with your mama than marry. I speak as I find."

"And so do I," said Sophia, pushed to endurance by the man's impertinence. "You think I just sit at home waiting for gentlemen to call and make their attentions to me? You, sir, are a fool indeed if you believe such a thing! I'll have you know I—"

"What?" interrupted Orlando, taking a step closer to her, so close his hand brushed against hers. "Gallivant about the Town, looking for suitors? Send notes of enquiry to eligible bachelors? Take out advertisements in the papers seeking a husband?"

Sophia flushed. As if she would ever do such a thing!

"No," she said darkly. "But I certainly do not accost people as you do, insult them for no reason, then expect them to be impressed!"

Orlando flinched, and Sophia congratulated herself on finally hitting home. Well, she could not permit the man to simply speak to her however he wanted! After all, the arrow about her being the youngest had certainly pierced her heart.

The youngest Fitzroy. The youngest of six sisters, and twelve cousins…it had been more than she could bear before she had entered Society. Always left out, always left behind, Sophia had hated being the youngest ever since she could remember. The last thing she needed was handsome—was *irritating* gentlemen pointing that out in Almack's.

"You know, Miss Fitzroy, I must admit, I am rather impressed by you."

Sophia blinked. Had those words really come out of Orlando

Dunbar's mouth?

"See, now I have surprised you," he said with a grin. "No, I am not one to hold on to false ideas if proven wrong. And I must tell you, Sophia—"

"Do not call me that," Sophia cut in, cheeks once again heating.

It was outrageous! Orlando—Mr. Dunbar; she should really think of him as Mr. Dunbar—had no right to speak to her with her first name. As though they were lovers.

At once the image of Orlando pulling her into his arms, embracing her, kissing her, rushed into Sophia's mind. A wonderful image, a scintillating one, one that returned that rush of heat through her body.

Sophia hastily pushed it aside. She was not going to permit herself to be overwhelmed.

"Fine," said Orlando, lowering his voice yet not looking away from her eyes. "I must tell you, Miss Fitzroy, that I rarely change my mind or find myself proven wrong. The fact that you have done both in one conversation is remarkable."

It was difficult not to preen at this pronouncement. Remarkable. She was remarkable.

Sophia saw a grin slip across Orlando's face, and swiftly reminded herself she did not want to impress him. Had no desire, whatsoever, to continue this conversation.

So why was she still here, standing by him, looking into those sparkling green eyes?

"And now I want to dance with you," said Orlando in that same low, intimate voice. "Damn, Miss Fitzroy. What have you done to me?"

Sophia swallowed. Well, she *had* wished for a scandalous romance, and there would be nothing so scandalous as taking to the dance floor at Almack's with a gentleman she did not really know, had never been introduced to, and without the approval of either of her parents.

The temptation flickered in her heart.

"What I really want is a scandalous romance."

"Well, what a shame," Sophia said lightly, smiling as brightly as she could. "For I have no interest in dancing with you."

Ignoring the astonished jaw drop of her conversational partner, she turned away from Orlando Dunbar and walked calmly away, carefully navigating her way through the crowd.

And she did not look back. Despite all her instincts telling her to see whether Orlando was still looking at her, Sophia did not look back.

CHAPTER TWO

"—WHICH IS CERTAINLY not the way we raised you!"

Sophia sighed heavily, trying as best she could to suffer through the indignity of being told off like a child who had stolen an apple from a cart.

"And that is not the reaction I would expect from a young lady who spoke so boldly and so scandalously to a gentleman at Almack's!"

Arthur Fitzroy was glaring at his youngest daughter, who was curled up in an armchair by the fire, and Sophia had the good grace to look a little bashful.

Well, she could not entirely refute the truth of her father's words. She had spoken to Orlando—to Mr. Dunbar rather rudely, and in plain view of all who were there. Though, honestly, she had not expected the news to get back to her parents so quickly.

The morning after her unexpected conversation with the gentleman who set her heart racing, even if she would not admit it, her parents had sat her down for a serious word.

Sophia swallowed. Her conversation with Mr. Dunbar had been taken entirely the wrong way. If they were going to get their information from Caroline, that was to be expected!

"I do not see what the problem is, truly," she said with another sigh. "I spoke to a gentleman, he spoke to me, and that was it. It is not as though I—I did something scandalous!"

Despite great temptation, Sophia thought as her mother raised an eyebrow.

After all, it would have been wildly pleasant to have danced with Orlando Dunbar. Though she had no evidence for this supposition, Sophia was certain he would have been an excellent dancer: in time, elegant, and when he took her hand...

Sophia cleared her throat and sat a little straighter. She had done no such thing, and really, she thought she was to be congratulated! Did her parents have any idea how odd it was to be here, living with them, after five sisters had filled the place with noise, laughter, games, gossip, joy?

And she had turned down the opportunity to dance with a handsome and intriguing—and irritating—gentleman.

"If I had danced with Orlando—with Mr. Dunbar," Sophia corrected herself hastily, "you would have said it was outrageous for me to dance with someone I had not been introduced to! So what was I supposed to do?"

"You were not supposed to *speak* to gentlemen you had not been introduced to," said Selina with a wry smile. "You know that, Sophia—do not feign ignorance."

Sophia clenched her jaw. *Yes, yes, all these rules and regulations*—if she had to guess, all the rules of Society were designed to keep gentlemen and ladies away from each other, rather than bring them together!

How was she supposed to have a scandalous romance, as her sisters had done, if she could not even talk to a gentleman?

"Mr. Dunbar?"

Sophia turned to her father, who had been pacing up and down the room, but was now standing by the window. He had a confused expression on his face.

"Yes, that is what I said," Sophia replied, perhaps more defensively than was required. How long was she going to sit through this lecture?

"I do not know a Mr. Dunbar," said her father slowly. "Most odd. I thought I was at least vaguely acquainted with most of the reputable men in Town."

Sophia leaned forward eagerly. "Does that mean he is disreputable?"

"Sophia!"

"I want a little adventure in my life," said Sophia with a grin at her mother, who looked just as scandalized as Caroline had. "All this sitting around and waiting for life to happen—"

"I thought I heard your voice," said her sister Arabella, entering the room with a wry smile on her face. "What have you done this time?"

"What do you mean, what have I—What did Caroline say?" Sophia said defensively.

That was the trouble with large families, of course: everything one did immediately got passed around. It was impossible to keep anything quiet.

Arabella, perhaps the gentlest of the Fitzroy sisters, raised an eyebrow as she removed her pelisse and bonnet and threw both onto the sofa. "Should I have heard from Caroline?"

"No," said Sophia quickly.

"Your sister," said their mother with a wry smile, "was seen at Almack's last night talking—nay, *debating*—with a gentleman to whom she was not introduced. More, your father does not even recognize his name."

Arabella's eyes widened as she sat beside her mother. "Sophia Fitzroy!"

Sophia groaned. She had wanted the lecture to be over, not extended or expanded!

It was intolerable, this critique of her actions, her reputation, her goings-on... Could she not just slip away with a handsome stranger, be kissed silly, then return home for dinner?

"It was just a conversation," she said wearily. "Honestly, I think this has all been blown far out of proportion. Mr. Dunbar—"

"Dunbar?" Arabella interrupted, her face going pale. "Not...not Orlando Dunbar?"

Sophia stared. *Arabella?* Arabella knowing who Orlando was, and not her father? It was unheard of. Arabella's husband Nathaniel was hardly a recluse, but at the same time, he hated Town, preferring to spend almost all the year at his country estate. They barely saw him, and Arabella was so besotted with him, and their three children, that the London Fitzroys hardly saw her either.

How had she heard of Orlando—of Mr. Dunbar if their father hadn't?

Arthur turned to his daughter. "You know of this Mr. Dunbar?"

"I most certainly do not," said Arabella with a dry laugh, "but I do know his lordship, Orlando Matthew Dunbar, Viscount Dunbar!"

Sophia's mouth fell open.

"What would you know about titles?"

"Oh, I know everything that goes on here. I know all about you."

Oh, she had made a complete fool of herself—and before a handsome viscount, too!

"Viscount Dunbar?" repeated their mother.

Sophia tried hard not to roll her eyes. Trust her mother to be immediately swayed by the mere presence of a title.

"Title or not, I do not see why I should not talk to him," she said firmly.

"Well, I do," said Arabella.

The entire room turned to her, and Sophia leaned forward in her seat. What did her sister know about this Viscount Dunbar?

"You think it not worth our time seeking out his acquaintance?" asked their papa.

"I would stay as far away from that gentleman as possible," said Arabella darkly. "The Viscount Dunbar has a terrible reputation—a very scandalous man, bedding many...I mean," she corrected herself hastily, glancing at Sophia, "he is not safe for young ladies to be around."

Bedding many...lovers. That was surely what her sister was going to say, thought Sophia wildly. A rake! A rascal, not just a cad, but a scoundrel too.

"And now I want to dance with you. Damn, Miss Fitzroy. What have you done to me?"

Goodness—to think she had been merely a decision away from stepping onto the dance floor at Almack's with a rake, right before the good and great of the *ton*. She'd had a lucky escape—Sophia was certain that was what her family believed.

But her heart twisted painfully, regret searing across her chest. Dancing with Orlando Dunbar, viscount, rake, seducer of ladies, would have been far more exciting than anything else she had done for weeks.

A scandalous romance? She would have appeared in the scandal sheets just for standing up with him.

Disappointment flooded her mind as Sophia considered what could have been, if she had just had the bravery to stand up with a man to whom she had not been introduced. Why, she had been seeking a love affair, had she not? Whether she was serious about her words or not, Orlando could certainly have given her something to think about.

She remembered the curve of his smile, that very knowing smile as he had beheld her, and shivered. There was a gentleman who knew how to please a woman.

"Just what kind of scandals—" Sophia began, but her father cut her off.

"No, Sophia, I do not believe it appropriate for you to know such things," he said sternly. "You have already had far more to do with this Viscount Dunbar than I think fitting. We have your reputation to think of, after all, for if you marry."

If you marry. *Not* when.

Sophia tried hard not to think about what Orlando had said only the night before.

"If you ask me, Miss Fitzroy, you, like all youngest sisters, are more likely to stay a spinster with your mama than marry."

Was that what her parents were hoping, that she would never wed and stay with them? Look after them, play whist with them, accompany them to card parties and dull dinners?

Sophia's heart twisted. No. That was not her fate. Not if she could help it.

"I did not dance with him and have no intention of seeking the man out," she said with a sigh. "Is that it? Can I go now? I have a little Christmas shopping I wish to do before—"

"You are going to stay right here," her mother said firmly.

"But Mama!"

"Your mother is right," said Arthur heavily. "Do not look at me like that. The last thing we need is for the gossips of London to see you gallivanting out in public on your own."

Sophia looked instinctively at her sister. "Arabella can accompany—"

"I was actually going to return home," Arabella said apologetically. "I have someone coming in the next hour with samples of new wallpapers for me to consider."

"In the Japanese style?" asked their mother eagerly. "May I accompany you? I was thinking of redecorating the dining room, or one of the bedchambers now the girls have left."

Sophia seethed in her armchair. *Now the girls have left*—did her mother think it entirely impossible, then, that *she* would ever leave to get married?

"I will come with you," said her papa, "or else my darling wife may order far more than—"

"You mean to tell me you are *all* going?" cried Sophia in disbelief.

Arabella had already risen from her seat and started pulling on her pelisse before she answered. "Well, I cannot help that, Sophia, can I?"

"You stay here," said their mother with a warning frown as she followed her daughter. "I mean it, Sophia."

"And I will know if you have been out," Arthur said with a laugh as he moved to the door. "Have a lovely morning, Sophia—perhaps afternoon as well. We may stay for lunch."

"But—"

The door shut behind her family before Sophia could say another word. As she continued to seethe in the armchair, she heard a few more pattering phrases about what to wear, just how cold it was out there, whether it would snow today, or before Christmas at the very least, then her sister and parents' voices disappeared as the front door closed.

Well! Sophia rose instantly from the armchair, unable to stay still a moment longer. How dare they just abandon her to an entire day at home—not even an invitation to look at Arabella's poxy wallpapers! Not that she really wished to see them.

Sophia moved to the window seat, her usual position in the drawing room, and looked wistfully out onto the street beyond.

It was most unfair. It was not as though she had done something actually wrong! All she had done was speak plainly and directly to a gentleman she did not know. Was that a crime?

"Well, what a shame. For I have no interest in dancing with you."

Sophia swallowed. It was not a crime, but it was certainly beyond the bounds of reasonable decorum. Perhaps that was why she had enjoyed it so much.

An entire day at home, without anyone to entertain her or her to entertain. *Not much different from every day,* Sophia thought bitterly. She leaned back, lying on the window seat and looking up at the ceiling. How was she to wile away the time until luncheon, then?

Sophia's eyelashes fluttered closed. She knew how she wished to spend it: thinking about Orlando.

Discovering he was both a viscount and a rake of the first degree was rather thrilling, in a way—though she was relieved to have been ignorant last night.

She had never spoken to a rake before. Her mother had seen to it she was never introduced to anyone who could possibly be described in that manner, so Sophia had to satiate her hunger for gossip through the scandal sheets.

A face appeared in her mind's eye. A face she certainly should not be thinking of.

"I must tell you, Miss Fitzroy, that I rarely change my mind or find myself proven wrong. The fact that you have done both in one conversation is remarkable."

Sophia smiled as his handsome face smiled, a smile that was all too knowing—precisely the sort of smile her mother would not like her to receive. A smile that made Sophia feel…well, *feel*. Feel everything, every breath of wind on her skin, her heart beating faster, warmth spreading throughout her body…

A loud knocking at the front door made Sophia jerk upright, face warm at the idea that someone could find her lying there, thinking of such a handsome man when she certainly had no right to.

From her seat by the window, she could just make out a figure by the door. A gentleman's great coat, a top hat edged with blue ribbon, and a most haughty air. Certainly not a gentleman she had ever seen before.

Curiosity flickered at the edges of Sophia's heart. Who was it?

Another loud rapping echoed around the house, the noise seeping in under the door. Well, Mrs. Castle did not appear to be willing to answer it—she was likely somewhere else in the house, unable to hear it.

Sophia rose to her feet. If no one else was going to do it…

It took but a moment to step across the hallway and reach the front door. And she wasn't doing anything wrong, precisely, Sophia told herself. Her parents had told her to stay at home, and that was what she was doing.

They hadn't said anything about being forbidden to answer the door.

Only when Sophia pulled it open and saw who was standing on the doorstep did she realize that perhaps she had obeyed the letter of the law but not the spirit of it—for right there before her was the very rakish scoundrel her parents had been so eager to keep her from.

"Ah, Miss Fitzroy," said Viscount Orlando Dunbar smoothly. "Good morning."

"What on earth are you doing here?" Sophia could not help but blurt out.

Heat seared her cheeks, and her gaze dropped to her feet before she lifted it to meet his amused face.

It was a reasonable question! There was no reason why such a man would be calling on her—if he was calling on her, which she very much doubted. It was an error, of course. He was looking for another house.

"You refused to dance with me last night," he said quietly.

Sophia swallowed, then leaned against the doorframe without looking away from the delicious gentleman. "I did."

"Young ladies," Orlando said, his voice low, "do not say no to me."

A shiver rushed up Sophia's spine. Yes, that she could well believe; Orlando was a gentleman she thought any woman would say yes to, no matter the question.

The scandalous thought was, thankfully, not one she spoke aloud.

"Well, I am sorry to disappoint your *lordship*," Sophia said as haughtily as she was able. "But I did not wish to dance with you."

The lie tasted bitter on her tongue as she attempted not to be impressed by Orlando. Now she knew he was a rake, a seducer of ladies, she could see it in his eyes. It was not an easy thing to warn others about; it was more his air. The way he held himself. As though he always got what he wanted, no matter the cost.

"Ah," Orlando said with a rueful smile, "you have discovered my true identity, then."

"Why did you not tell me you were a viscount?" Sophia asked, knowing it was an impertinent question but certain her parents would be none the wiser. "I mean, all that guff you said about titles—"

"I said titles did not make the man, and I stand by that remark," said Orlando with a dry laugh. "There are plenty of gentlemen with titles who, I would say, are not deserving of five minutes of your time."

"Too true," said Sophia with a mischievous smile. "One of them is standing right before me."

What came over her to say such a thing, she did not know. Her impish wit was usually something she attempted to keep within the family, in case of accidental offending, but in this case she was rewarded for her boldness.

A wave of desire passed across Orlando's face, and then it was gone. If Sophia had not been examining him closely—to spot these things, she told herself, no other reason—she would have missed it.

"My word, you are a firebrand, aren't you?" he said softly. "Well, as you refused to dance with me then, you must dance with me now."

"Dance—dance now?" Sophia spluttered. The man was mad, quite mad! "I cannot—There is no music, no—I am not going to dance with you in the street!"

Yet she did not step away, close the door, and consider herself fortunate to have escaped the designing viscount's clutches.

No, Sophia was not going to leave the most exciting conversation she'd ever had in her life. Rake or not, Orlando was a gentleman she was drawn to, inexplicably—or perhaps explicably.

She tried not to look at the broad shoulders, the clean jaw, the way his eyes sparkled.

She was not going to be overwhelmed.

"I can make it worth your while," Orlando said softly.

Sophia swallowed, hoping her cheeks were not flushing. Most of her conversations with gentlemen had been limited to three safe topics her mother had drilled into her: weather, fashion, and how pleasant the occasion was. It didn't matter whether it was card party, dinner, ball, picnic—the occasion was always *pleasant*.

But this wasn't pleasant. This was wild, scandalous, impossible. She certainly shouldn't be prolonging the conversation...yet she appeared unable to step away.

"I shouldn't even be talking to you."

"Why?" Orlando advanced up the steps to stand right before

her, only inches away. "Because I am a rake? Because I bed ladies far more often than I talk to them? Because I am in danger very much of kissing you now, of taking your innocence and hearing you beg for more?"

Sophia stared, unable to take it all in. *Such words—such words should not be spoken!*

Yet she craved them, wanted more, wanted to know precisely what he would do to her, how he would kiss her. Oh, if only he would kiss her...

"Perhaps," she managed to say, "but as I am not interested in such—such lewd suggestions, you may go."

Sophia blinked up into the green, dazzling eyes of Viscount Orlando Dunbar. *Not interested...* Nothing could be further from the truth. But she would not risk her reputation entirely; a scandalous romance, that was what she had wanted. Not an entirely lost reputation.

"My, my, Sophia Fitzroy," Orlando murmured, and Sophia tried not to look at the distracting way his lips moved. "You have just given me a challenge."

Sophia swallowed. It was precisely the opposite of what she had intended. "Well, my lord," she said bracingly, "I suppose the first part of your challenge will be how to walk through walls."

"What do you—"

Sophia swiftly stepped back and closed the door in his face.

Heart racing, hardly able to believe she had done such a thing, she waited silently.

A laugh. A chuckle. She could imagine Orlando shaking his head wryly at the sudden way she had departed, and then footsteps grew quieter and quieter.

Sophia leaned her forehead against the door and tried to catch her breath. What had she done?

CHAPTER THREE

"HERE WE ARE!"

The carriage pulled up outside the large and impressive townhouse, and Sophia leaned to the window to attempt to see the top. It was impossible; Caroline and Stuart's London residence was at least four times the size of the Fitzroy family home, and from the carriage it was difficult to see the upmost floor.

"Such a lovely idea for your sister to host a Christmas ball," Selina said, patting her hair carefully as though the pins were dislodged in the short carriage ride. "Do not you think?"

Sophia swallowed and was very careful not to say precisely what she thought.

Namely, that she was well aware the ball was hosted partly for Caroline to show off to the family, partly to impress London Society, and lastly…

She grimaced. Lastly, to push her in the way of eligible young gentlemen who had no conversation, no spirit, and therefore held no interest for her.

"Lovely," Sophia lied sweetly, beaming at her parents. "Shall we?"

She was eager to get inside. It was freezing in the carriage, with the December air pulling a chill right through it, and as soon as Sophia stepped onto the pavement, she could hear the music from inside the house. That had to be better than standing out here in the cold.

"There you are. I thought you would never get here—Careful, Victoria, do not push your sister's... Ah, she cannot hear me now anyway," said Arabella distractedly in the hall, smiling wearily at her parents as her children scampered away from her. "When did we start to listen to you, Mama?"

"I am still waiting for that happy event," said Selina wryly. "I did not know Caroline had permitted the children to attend!"

"It was that, or leave them in absolute tears, and how could I do such a thing?" said Arabella fretfully as Sophia allowed a footman in Cheshire livery to remove her pelisse. "Sophia, you look...nice."

Sophia glared at her sister, but saw in an instant it was sheer exhaustion that had made her hesitate. "Thank you."

And she did look nice, if she said so herself. Lucy had left behind her favorite green silk gown when she married a few years ago, its sprigs of embroidered holly were perfect for a Christmas ball, and Sophia had never worn it before.

It felt...special. Different. As though special and different things would occur this evening, merely because she was wearing it.

"My, my, Sophia Fitzroy. You have just given me a challenge."

Sophia shivered, despite the warmth of the hall. She was not going to permit that blackguard, that *Dunbar*, to ruin her evening with her family.

Just because he went around saying such terrible things to young ladies, she told herself as more of her sisters appeared and embraced their parents. Just because Orlando—the Viscount Dunbar—thought it appropriate to say such things to ladies he barely knew!

That did not mean she was going to pay him any heed. Any heed whatsoever.

Sophia swallowed. If only that were true. The blasted man had been in her thoughts almost every moment since she had last seen him, just a few days ago. But she was here for Caroline's ball, and that was what she should focus on.

"—never seen such decorations. You must come into the ballroom, Mama," Esther was saying with a look of astonishment. "Why, I do not think, even at Kendal…"

It was all Sophia could do not to grin as the Fitzroys stepped to the ballroom. Yes, Esther had always been the peacekeeper of the family; even though she was now a duchess, she would never dream of being more impressive than her sister, the countess.

"Goodness…" Sophia breathed.

Despite herself, it was impossible not to marvel at the effort Caroline had gone to for the Christmas ball.

The ballroom was covered, almost lined, with decorations. Holly and ivy, ribbons, candles, but also what appeared to be glass ornaments that looked like snowflakes, glittering and shimmering in the candlelight.

Trays upon trays of food lined the console tables around the edges of the room, with breaks for punch tables, and a small platform at one end where a group of musicians were playing a country dance.

Footmen in Cheshire livery meandered about the place, topping up guests' glasses and retrieving empty ones from those who wished to dance.

Excited murmurs echoed around the room as the Fitzroy family entered. Sophia attempted not to preen. It was pleasant to be a part of this family sometimes.

"Mama, Papa, welcome!" Caroline glided over, resplendent in a gown with more golden embroidery than Sophia had ever seen, and diamond earrings glittering underneath a tower of feathers. "Come, let me introduce you to some very interesting…"

Sophia tried hard not to sigh. *Of course.*

This was not just a ball, not just a chance to show off the only unmarried Fitzroy sister…it was a chance for Caroline to "help" the family.

"But you don't know the best people!" she would often say,

aghast as one or both of her parents admitted that they had never met Lord So-and-so, or hosted Lady What's-her-face. "Lady Romeril! You must have been introduced—you simply must know the best people!"

"The people we already know we consider to be the best," their papa had gently reminded her only last week...but it appeared his words had not sunk in.

Casting Sophia a despairing look, Arthur and Selina were rushed off to be introduced to people she thought looked rather smug and stuck-up, leaving her with two of her sisters, Lucy and Jemima.

"You look lovely," said Jemima stiffly. "I—"

Then, without another word, Sophia's sister rushed off, leaving her two sisters looking after her in confusion.

"What was all that about?" asked Lucy in wonder.

Sophia shook her head. "I have no idea."

"Wait, isn't that my gown?"

Sophia looked down quickly at the green holly gown she had put on with such pleasure. "Maybe," she said defensively as the dance ended and people around them applauded. "I found it in your bedchamber after you were married, and—"

"That's my gown, you minx!"

"If I am not keeping you in sufficient gowns, you must tell me," said Percy, Lucy's husband, as he came to his sister-in-law's rescue with a wink. "Come now, let us dance."

"You only wish to get your hands on me."

"Don't tell them..."

Sophia made a face as her sister was led away by her husband. Did they have to be so...so blatant with their affection? She was absolutely not jealous. Not at all. Why care if all five of her sisters were adored, and she was not?

"Aunty Sophie."

Sophia looked down. Arabella's eldest, Victoria, was gazing up with curiosity.

"Yes?" said Sophia, crouching to her haunches to look into

the child's eyes.

Her niece frowned, as though the question she needed to ask was remarkably complicated, then said slowly, "My mama is married."

Sophia's heart sank slowly. *Oh, goodness.* She certainly had not expected to have this sort of conversation with a four-year-old. Could not Arabella have asked her housekeeper to look after the child, rather than bring her?

Glancing up, she could see neither Arabella nor her husband, Nathaniel, to rescue her.

"Aunty Sophie."

"Yes?" Sophia said distractedly. Perhaps if she could gain the attention of her mother, Selina could rescue Sophia from her granddaughter…

"And all my other aunts are married."

Sophia swallowed. *Ah.* So it was not a question about…about that.

Victoria blinked innocently up at her aunt. "So why are you not married?"

Sophia sighed. That was an excellent question, though not one she was willing to explore with a child. "You know, I think it is because of…the tickle monster."

Victoria's eyes widened in disbelief. "There's no such thing as a—"

"There she comes!"

Squealing delightedly, Victoria scampered through the crowd in the ballroom as Sophia chased after her, making the wild, nonsensical noises of the tickle monster her father had created years ago.

"Oh, I'm coming to get you! I'm going to eat you and tickle you and—Ouch!"

Sophia had literally run headlong into someone.

"Damn!" the person she had run into said under his breath. Victoria was nowhere to be seen.

Sophia straightened up, furious at being caught doing such a wild thing in public, and saw with absolute horror...it was Orlando.

"Miss Sophia Fitzroy," he said, rubbing his arm where she had collided with him. "You have a rather interesting habit of being entirely unexpected."

Her lungs were tight, and she was hardly able to breathe, and Sophia knew she should say something, anything, but it was impossible. There he was, just as she remembered him, tall, handsome, charming...

Not charming, Sophia told herself sternly as she brushed down her gown and looked defiantly back up at him. *Not charming at all.* "Wh-what are you doing here?"

She could feel the flush coming, rising from her toes up her legs, into her chest...soon it would reach her face, and he would know just how mortified she was!

When she finally managed to look into Orlando's eyes, Sophia was astonished to see he was smiling.

"Here?"

Sophia glanced around the ballroom, to where a line of couples were dancing elegantly in the middle. "Here. My sister's Christmas ball—only people who are invited—"

"I was invited," said Orlando smoothly, stepping toward her.

Taking a step backward was a challenge at a ball, but thankfully, Sophia did not step on any toes as she hastily moved away. She was experiencing far too much of a reaction just being this close to him—the last thing she needed was to feel more of his presence, more of that hot masculinity.

No, she needed to stay well away from him. So why was she still standing here, talking to him?

"What are you doing here?" he asked.

Sophia's irritation flared. "What do you mean, what I am doing here? This is my sister's ball!"

"That is the funny thing about sisters, isn't it?" Orlando said as though he were an expert on all sisters in general, and Fitzroy sisters in particular. "Siblinghood does not always guarantee one an invitation."

Sophia swallowed. It was most unfair that Orlando—that the Viscount Dunbar was here, looking handsome. His jaw was grazed with a light dusting of beard, as though he had decided not to shave for a few days, and his green eyes still glittered.

Which I certainly did not notice, she told herself firmly. Because she had no interest in the man. The rake. A scandalous man.

"What I really want is a scandalous romance."

Yes, she had said that, but she had not meant…this. An actual scandal, if she was seen talking too long to a man with a reputation such as his.

"Well," Sophia said awkwardly, "good evening, your lord—"

"Are you finally going to accept my hand for a dance?"

Heat sparked in Sophia's chest. "Absolutely not! You are the very last person I would ever—"

"Ah, good," said Lucy distractedly, rushing past them, looking a little gray, "you've found someone to dance with. Well done, Sophia."

Without even asking whether or not the gentleman wished to dance with her sister, Lucy took Orlando's hand without a shred of embarrassment, thrust it into Sophia's, then meandered away.

Sophia stared at the connection between them. His large hand enclosed hers—thankfully he was wearing a glove, but that did not prevent her feeling the intense heat radiating through each and every finger.

She was holding the hand of Viscount Orlando Dunbar. The rake. The scoundrel. The gentleman who made her so warm it was almost uncomfortable, yet she would not change this sensation for anything.

Sophia knew what she should do. Pull away her hand, give Orlando an imperious look, glare, if possible, then stalk away after making a rather cutting remark.

She lifted her gaze to meet his, ready to do just that. "I…ah…"

"Excellent," said Orlando. "Come on."

"No, wait—"

It did not appear to matter that she had no wish to dance with the handsome rascal; Sophia found her hand clasped so tightly she could not free herself. She had to endure the indignity of being pulled forward past friends, past family, past strangers who whispered swiftly at the sight of her hand in hand with such a blackguard…

And then she was standing in the set, opposite a man who made her feel…

Sophia swallowed. This was not what she had planned for such an evening.

"I am intrigued to see how you dance, Miss Fitzroy," said Orlando with a bow.

Sophia almost laughed. Well, fortunately for him, she was unlikely to lose her footing in this scenario, at least. That was one of the benefits of having five older sisters: she had been practicing almost every dance for years. She could do a few with her eyes shut.

Not that she wished to do such a thing here. Not if that meant missing out on one second of looking at Orlando.

"I am intrigued to know why you still wish to dance with me at all," she admitted, stepping elegantly to the left and twisting as the dance began.

Orlando laughed. "Why, you don't think I want ladies flocking to me for a title, or my wealth, or any of that nonsense, do you?"

Sophia tried not to think about it but could not help it. Title, wealth…and scandal, of course.

"And you, Miss Fitzroy…you are different."

The words were breathed rather than spoken, and Sophia gasped as Orlando came up beside her and escorted her down the line of dancers. He was so close, his hands on her waist, and she had not even had a moment to prepare herself for the intimacy.

His scent filled her mind, intoxicating her far more than the sherry her father let her taste, his hands scalding on her waist, branding her, and a lurch twisted her stomach that was nonetheless...*pleasant.*

What was this man doing to her?

"Different?"

"You did not chase after me, flock to me, seek me out," Orlando said quietly as they separated, returning to their lines.

His gaze was molten, and Sophia thought for a moment she would melt under it. What had she done? Attracted the attention of the most scandalous rake in all of London...and now he was interested in her?

"And...and why do they flock to you at all?" she asked, attempting to be defiant.

A twinkle glittered in Orlando's eye. "Why do you think?"

Sophia swallowed as she stepped forward as the dance dictated, offering up her hands to him, though the last—and first—thing she wished to do was hold his hands.

Her instincts were right. A shiver of pleasure rushed down her spine as her hands were taken by Orlando... The way he looked at her, as though he could see right through her...as though he could see through her clothes.

Sophia blanched as she turned to the lady beside her, hoping to goodness the outrageous thought that had flitted through her mind could not be read on her face.

It was a nonsense, after all. Orlando—the Viscount Dunbar was not interested in her for...for that! He had to know, surely, that she was by no means unprotected, with a prominent family who loved her and who would take great umbrage at the deflowering of their last daughter!

And yet...

"I have heard much about you, Viscount Dunbar."

Orlando groaned as they stepped foward, his hands once more on her waist. "I want you to call me Orlando," he whispered in her ear.

"I expect very many ladies call you Orlando," Sophia quipped, heart pounding. "Very many, if the rumors I have heard about you are correct."

She thought for a moment she had gone too far, uttered something far too scandalous for a young lady with her standing.

A flash of a grin appeared on Orlando's face as he released her. "Very many?"

"In fact," said Sophia, emboldened by his reply, "I have even heard you currently have not one, but three French mistresses!"

Mrs. Castle, their housekeeper, was a mine of information.

If she had thought to embarrass him, Sophia could not have been more incorrect.

Orlando grinned, winking as they stepped to the right around the twirling couple beside them. "Oh, at least three."

Sophia flushed, heat searing her cheeks, and he laughed. If only she did not show her emotions so easily. It was something she had always fought against.

"Yes, three mistresses at the moment, for who could truly satisfy me?" Orlando said, his smile only growing. "My three French hens."

Three French hens.

It was impossible to take such a man seriously. If half the rumors Mrs. Castle had suggested were true, Orlando Dunbar was a man not to be trusted.

Yet...there was something about him. Something that drew Sophia to him, not merely because she wanted to feel the touch of his hands on her waist, but something deeper. Darker. Far more interesting.

"Tell me about them," she found herself saying.

It was a disgraceful thing to say, but Sophia could not take back her words—and it appeared Orlando was scandalized.

His mouth fell open before he managed to collect himself. "You...you want to know about my three French hens?"

"I do," said Sophia. It was rather pleasant to see the handsome man on the back foot. "What, you think young ladies do not...do not think of such things?"

"Do *you* think of such things?"

Sophia swallowed, glancing away for just a moment but finding her gaze drawn inexplicably back. She did think of such things—longed for the kiss of a man who loved her, the caresses that would drive her toward pleasure, toward something deeper and darker than she had ever known.

And Orlando was a man who could do just that, she was sure. One could tell just by looking at him that none of his mistresses were unsatisfied.

"Perhaps I do," she breathed.

Orlando groaned as they separated in the dance, bowing and curtseying to each other as the dance ended. "You are certainly not what I expected, Miss Fitzroy."

"Well, you know what they say," she said with a mischievous grin. "You cannot always believe the rumors."

CHAPTER FOUR

SOPHIA COULD NOT take it anymore.

She had been patient. She had waited. She had even asked a leading question of her sister not half an hour ago, but Arabella appeared to be entirely fixated on her embroidery.

Why had Arabella even come to visit the Fitzroys, leaving her children at home, if she was not going to talk!

Sophia looked up from the book she had been attempting to read for the last ten minutes without taking in a word, and glared at her older sister.

Well, had she not made it obvious enough? Had she not asked, relatively directly, about the gentleman who had been entirely clouding her thoughts since the ball yesterday?

"You are certainly not what I expected, Miss Fitzroy."

Sophia swallowed and looked at the crackling fire in the grate. It was most irritating for her sister not to willingly volunteer information about the viscount when she was so desperate to know whether Mrs. Castle's murmurs about him were true.

"Yes, three mistresses at the moment, for who could truly satisfy me? My three French hens."

Sophia certainly could not ask her mother, and she would not ask her father. But Arabella…she knew about Viscount Dunbar, and Sophia was determined to hear it. All of it.

"Arabella," Sophia said as an opening gambit.

Her sister looked up from her embroidery—a swallow on a blue background—with a faraway look. "Sophia."

Sophia smiled weakly. That was the trouble with Arabella. It was not that she was unintelligent—arguably she was the cleverest of all the Fitzroy sisters, perhaps of all the Fitzroy cousins. Still. She made you work for any conversation.

"You said before that the Viscount...the Viscount Dunbar had a terrible reputation."

Arabella nodded and wordlessly returned to her embroidery.

Sophia sighed and laid aside her book. "Come on, Bels, you know what I am asking!"

"And yet you do not ask," said Arabella with a wry smile. "You are as bad as Nathaniel, always thinking everyone understands precisely what you are thinking."

"Yes, I am sure it is very annoying," said Sophia dryly.

Her sister laughed. "You know, when one of the swans was sickened, Nathaniel never mentioned to me that—"

"But this Orlando," persisted Sophia, feeling a flush on her cheeks. "Viscount Dunbar, I mean. He could not have done anything that dreadful, not really."

Arabella raised an eyebrow, still focused on her swallow. "What makes you say that?"

"Well...Caroline invited him to her Christmas ball."

"Caroline did nothing of the sort," said Arabella darkly.

Sophia sat bolt upright in her armchair. She did not—Orlando had not been invited?

"What are you doing here?"

"What do you mean, what I am doing here? This is my sister's ball!"

It was outrageous, it was ridiculous—it was bold indeed to appear at an earl's private ball without an invitation! What had the man been thinking?

A desperate hope that he had done such a thing merely because he wished to see her flashed through Sophia's mind, but she pushed it aside immediately. No, she would not attempt to fool herself. There was no possibility he could have done such a thing. She was not a lightskirt, willing to accept his advances as perhaps so many others had.

So what had he meant by it?

"I-I did not know that," she stammered, trying to keep her voice level. "So Caroline does not like him, then?"

"I did not say that," Arabella replied. "Indeed, I do not believe there is a woman alive who can say that they truly dislike the Viscount Dunbar. It is more...well, his reputation."

Sophia nodded, hardly daring to break her sister's flow.

"It is absolutely awful," said Arabella finally, lifting her gaze from her embroidery and looking wide-eyed at her sister. "Truly, Sophia, I think it best I say nothing to you—"

"I need to know though, for—for my own protection," said Sophia, inventing wildly, heart racing in her chest. "So I know precisely why to avoid him."

Arabella smiled wryly. "I am not Mama, you know. You do not need to try that old trick with me."

Sophia's mouth fell open. "Old?"

"I believe Jemima tried that very trick, years ago, when you were little," said Arabella. "But your viscount—"

"He is not my viscount!" Sophia said hotly.

"Your viscount has seduced more ladies of the *ton* than I think all the rest of them combined," said Arabella, lowering her voice as though they could be overheard, though the drawing room was empty. "Oh, Sophia, the tales I could tell...ladies he has seduced, daughters he has ruined, widows he has... Well. And, of course, he always has three French mistresses. When he tires of one, he merely replaces her with another. *There* is a gentleman who knows what he wants."

Sophia swallowed, tasting the desire in her mouth. *A gentleman who knows what he wants*—and he wanted her.

At least, he had wanted to dance with her. Now she had finally been forced into it, she supposed Orlando was tired of her already and would undoubtedly leave her alone.

And it is not as though I wish to be one of the many ladies on his list, Sophia told herself hurriedly. Far from it. No, if she was going to be bedded by the Viscount Dunbar, it would have to mean something.

Mean something?

Sophia pushed the thought from her mind as sternly as she could. She was not going to permit herself to be bedded by anyone, let alone Orlando!

Even if he did make her whole body shiver when he touched her…

"Thankfully, however, your reputation precedes you."

Sophia jumped, startled. "I beg your pardon?"

Arabella shrugged. "Well, you are a Fitzroy. None of us have ever been caught—I mean, no scandal has ever been whispered about us, has it?"

Sophia narrowed her eyes at her sister. *Never been caught?* She knew it—she knew some of them, perhaps all of them, had got up to no good with their now-husbands. Was that what made the thought of scandal permissible, the fact her sisters had never been caught, and had then married the men who bedded them?

"No, you are far from his reaches, thank goodness," Arabella said, dropping her gaze to a particularly difficult part of the embroidery.

Sophia smiled weakly. *Yes, thank goodness.* Thank goodness a man like Orlando would never be interested in her; thank goodness he would never consider her seriously as a romantic partner. Thank goodness her life would continue as before, the same old thing, day after day unchanging.

"Anyway, I thought you were going to the concert."

Sophia glanced at the grandfather clock in the corner of the room and rose hastily to her feet, book falling to the floor. "Oh, no!"

"Take my carriage," called Arabella as Sophia rushed from the room. "But send it back!"

It really was most unlike her to forget such a thing, thought Sophia wildly as she pulled on a pelisse—Arabella's?—then rushed to the carriage waiting outside the house, adorned with the Cartier livery.

She had only agreed to attend the charity concert because her mama was unable to go. A prior engagement with Lady Romeril, she had told her daughter. And so Sophia had sent back her grateful acceptance, a genuine one too, and now she was going to be late!

Her heart was racing wildly as she stepped into the Duke of Axwick's home, following the pointed fingers of the footmen who smiled to see her rush down the corridor to the room that had been set aside for the concert.

Sophia could hear music seeping under the door as she reached it, heart thumping wildly, breath entirely lost.

"Miss?" said a footman with an arched eyebrow.

Trying to draw herself up and look like the elegant young lady she was supposed to be, Sophia smiled imperiously. "You may open the doors."

He did not precisely roll his eyes, but Sophia was almost certain she saw a sardonic look on the footman's face before he bowed and opened the door.

Mozart floated across the room as Sophia tried to quietly step inside, desperately looking for an empty chair, and spotted one right at the back on the end row. Relief seeping through her chest, she crept over, sat down, and breathed a huge sigh of relief.

"I thought you'd never get here."

Sophia almost fell off her chair. Orlando—the Viscount Dunbar was seated right beside her. Her leg was touching his, her hip grazing his own!

Her mouth fell open, and he chuckled under his breath. "Goodness, this entire day is a success now I have made you speechless."

"I—Not speech—*You!*" hissed Sophia.

It was all she could do to come up with those foolish words.

Her heart was racing so rapidly she could barely hear the music over the throb of her pulse in her ears—and that was not the only throb of which she was now aware.

There was something about being seated so close to a gentleman like Orlando, a gentleman who seemed able to undress a woman merely by looking at her, that made Sophia's body entirely unruly.

Heart racing, chest tight, desire rushing through her as it simply had no business doing, and that throb, that ache between her legs that simply did not make sense…

"Sophia?"

A horrible sense of dizziness rushed into Sophia's mind as she blinked, and Orlando's handsome visage faded in and out of view.

She had to get out of here. Charity concert or no charity concert, she could not stay.

"Sophia!"

Unsure precisely how her legs were able to carry her, but heartily glad they had not yet given way, Sophia managed to stumble to her feet and out of the room. The corridor swam before her eyes but the footman was gone, and there was no one there to—

"Easy does it."

Strong hands grasped her arms, steadying her, keeping her upright, and Sophia blinked up wildly at the person who had caught her.

Orlando Dunbar looked down into her eyes, no teasing laughter in his expression this time. It was almost like…concern? "Here, come along. There's a room you can sit in…"

He walked her carefully along the corridor and opened a door to what appeared to be a drawing room. Sophia stared as the viscount helped himself to the duke's home as though he did such a thing every day.

"Gently now."

Soft furnishings swallowed her up. Sophia blinked. She had been carefully placed on an elegant sofa in a room she did not recognize.

Orlando was kneeling before her, concern clearly visible on his face. "Sophia?"

Sophia blinked. The dizziness was gone, almost as abruptly as it had come, but it was replaced by a similar twisting nausea in her stomach. But it was not nausea, not dizziness. Something else.

"What are you doing here?"

Orlando chuckled. "You have got to stop asking me that."

"But...but you can't be here," Sophia said stupidly.

How was this possible? You went through life expecting to have handsome strangers sweep you off your feet, none of them did, and then all of a sudden, one could not move through Society without seeing the same one over and again.

"I most certainly am," Orlando said wryly. "How do you feel?"

"Feel?"

Sophia hardly knew how she felt. At least, she knew what she was feeling was most irregular, and certainly because of the handsome man before her. How dare he look at her like that, as if...as if he cared about her?

"You caught me."

"It was me or the floor."

Sophia had to smile. "I am sorry—thank you."

Orlando grinned and sat beside her on the sofa. "My pleasure. I always rather enjoy rescuing a damsel in distress."

"I am not in distress," Sophia said quickly.

Now her wits were starting to return, she realized just what situation she had managed to get herself into. She was alone, entirely alone, in a room she was not supposed to be in...with the Viscount Dunbar.

A more notorious scoundrel she could not find, apparently.

Sophia swallowed. "I did not expect you to be here."

"Well, I could hardly just abandon you, could I?" said Orlando lightly.

Trying not to notice just how close he was, Sophia tried to explain. "No, I mean…here. At the charity concert."

"And why not?"

Why not indeed? Sophia attempted to put it into words that would not offend. "I mean… Well. All your seducing and being a scoundrel—"

"A scoundrel?"

"I would have thought this was not your sort of thing at all," said Sophia with a laugh.

She had no choice but to speak openly; the presence of Orlando so close beside her did not appear to leave her any choice. There was something about him…something that drew out truth.

"My dear Miss Fitzroy," said Orlando slowly, taking her hand in his. "Who do you think is paying for all this?"

Sophia stared. What on earth did he mean?

His laughter made her flush. "Oh, I am glad to see I have surprised you—that is a gift in itself. No, I am afraid I am the benefactor of this little event. Oh, I convinced Axwick to put up for the room—my own place here in London is…well, not suitable for the general public. I paid for the musicians, the invitations, the generous donations…"

Sophia continued to stare. All the words made sense, individually, but coming together, out of Orlando's mouth?

No, surely not. This was hardly the picture of a rake, going through Society only interested in his own pleasure and getting his own way.

But…he was not lying. She could tell in the way he spoke proudly, if a little abashed, about how much work went into organizing a charitable concert. He truly was pleased to do it. He was proud, in fact, of being the founder of the whole thing.

"Well, I must say," Orlando concluded, "the entire thing was worth it, if I have impressed you just as much as your face is suggesting."

Sophia looked at her hands—one of which was inexplicably

entwined with Orlando's.

She gazed at the fingers, hardly able to tell which were his and which were her own. This gentleman, this man who surprised and confused and heightened all her senses without even a word. What was she supposed to think of a man like that? How was she supposed to understand her own heart when he made it flutter so wildly…

A hand, strong yet gentle, lifted up her chin so Sophia had no choice but to look into the eyes of Orlando Dunbar.

"Sophia Fitzroy," he said softly, green eyes fixed on hers, "if I have managed to surprise you half as much as you have surprised me, I have achieved something incredible."

Sophia swallowed, her heart skipping a beat, causing a ripple of desire.

She, surprise him? He was the one who had the reputation of a rake, who appeared to know precisely what it was that a woman wanted to hear. She supposed he had trotted out these lines before, easily winning over and charming those he wished to make love to.

Her gaze slipped to his lips, then back to his eyes, as desire pooled in her stomach. She must not stay here. She was alone, unchaperoned, with a man who… *Well.*

"In fact, I would go as far to say," said Orlando, his voice nothing more than a whisper now, "that I am almost surprised to admit that surprising you is the best thing that's happened to me all day."

She should leave. She should not stay here.

"Truly?" whispered Sophia.

Unaccountable though it was, for some reason she found herself leaning closer. Something about Orlando attracted her as no other man ever had, and she longed for him, felt the need to be close to him building in her, building to such a peak she could not ignore it.

"Orlando…" she breathed.

His eyes were hazed with desire, or lust, and he was leaning too; the distance between their lips was now only three inches…two inches…one inch…

Sophia had just allowed her eyelashes to fall, hardly able to believe she was about to experience her first ever kiss, when suddenly the connection was broken.

Even with her eyes shut, she knew Orlando had pulled back—the lack of his presence was a cold shower of disappointment—and his hand was wrenched from hers.

"Well then, Miss Sophia Fitzroy," said Orlando briskly.

Sophia opened her eyes to see him before her, a strange smile on his face as he stood rather awkwardly.

Very awkwardly. It was almost as though…

Heat seared her cheeks as she dropped her gaze hastily. She should not have been looking there—it was most unbecoming of her to even think of it—but now that she had seen the bulge of his manhood, taut and erect beneath his breeches, all for her, there was nothing else Sophia could think about.

He wanted her. He desired her, perhaps just as much as she desired him. Sophia had never had that effect on anyone before— at least, not knowingly.

And now she had made Orlando Dunbar want her. So why had he stepped away, not taken the kiss she offered? Why was he now, in fact, at least three feet away from her as though she could scald him if he got too close?

Though her heart was going a thousand miles an hour, Sophia tried to remain calm. "Orlando Dunbar."

"Are you ready to return to the concert?"

Unsure precisely whether she would be ready for anything ever again, let alone be able to stand, Sophia nodded. "I am ready."

She rose to her feet, found to her surprise they were able to hold her, and tried to smile at the man who was fast becoming the most intriguing part of the whole of London Society. What a Christmas this was turning out to be.

"In that case," said Orlando, rather formally, "I am delighted to escort you back."

Sophia only hesitated a moment before slipping her hand into his arm. "I…I do not know what you are doing to me."

The words had fallen from her lips before she could stop them, but for some reason, there was no smile of triumph on Orlando's face—no, quite to the contrary.

A wry smile twisted his mouth. "Strange. I was about to say the same thing to you."

CHAPTER FIVE

THE FINAL PIN was not settling in her hair, and Sophia was getting increasingly irritated.

"Do not worry, I will fix it," she said with a sigh, staring at her reflection in the looking glass and wishing a less ruffled Sophia could look back at her. "That will be all, Peters."

The lady's maid she shared with her mother bobbed a curtsey and left the room, abandoning Sophia both to the creation of a perfect look, and…

"I do not think I have ever seen you care so much about your appearance," came Lucy's teasing comment.

Sophia gritted her teeth and smiled at her sister's reflection. That was the trouble with sisters who felt they could come and go from the Fitzroy home as they pleased. This was her home now—but that did not stop them from meandering in and out.

"Do you not have somewhere to be?" she asked pointedly.

Lucy sighed, lounging on Sophia's bed. "I suppose I should return home at some point; Percy will be wondering where I am…but then, it has been so long since I have seen you."

"You saw me not two weeks ago, at Almack's," Sophia said distractedly.

All she needed was one more pin, and her hair would be perfect. And she had not spent so long on it so as to be called vain. At least, Sophia did not think so. True, she did not typically spend this amount of time trying to get every curl right, trying to affix every pin with care…but this was a special evening. An important one.

Because of the charitable nature of the ball, Sophia told herself sternly. Certainly not because a certain gentleman may be there. *Definitely* not because Orlando might be there.

"That was not the same, and you know it—we barely had any time to talk, and I want to hear all about the news of the Town," said Lucy petulantly.

There was a gentle laugh from Arabella, who had similarly invited herself into Sophia's bedchamber—if you could call it invited, as she had neither asked permission nor replied when Sophia asked what she was doing there. She was seated on the blanket box at the end of Sophia's bed.

"News of Town? Lucy Ardingley, you live in Town!"

"You know I am only just out again in Society after my confinement," Lucy said with a grin. "Goodness, I cannot think of anything duller than being forced to stay home all the time, unable to go out, unable to see anyone…"

Sophia allowed her sister's words to wash over her. She was not going to get ahead of herself, thinking that this night would be special for…for that particular reason.

No. No, she had no expectation of seeing the Viscount Dunbar at Lady Romeril's ball tonight, and moreover, she had no wish to.

She certainly had not been dreaming of him, dreaming of that moment when he almost kissed her. Dreaming of his hands in his, his finger lifting her chin, the sweeping way her stomach stirred as her whole body readied itself for him…

"And besides, I thought you hated Lady Romeril!"

"I don't hate Lady Romeril," Sophia said with a laugh, forcing the hairpin into place and turning to look at her sisters. "No one dares hate Lady Romeril."

"That is certainly true," said Lucy, grinning.

Arabella frowned at the pair of them. "You know it is terrible manners to speak of your betters in such a way."

"Of my elders, maybe, but I would not call Lady Romeril my better," said Lucy tartly. "Why, her sons are absolute cads. One of them spoke most rudely to Percy the other day, and I…"

Sophia tried to follow the story; Lucy always told them well, even if she did embellish them. For greater enjoyment, she always said. But it was hard to follow when completely different words were echoing around her mind.

"I…I do not know what you are doing to me."

"Strange. I was about to say the same thing to you."

Sophia shivered. She was *not* going to be seduced by Orlando Dunbar.

At least, not entirely. A few kisses would not hurt. Perhaps an embrace, an encounter in a dark alley…

"So why did you agree to go to this thing tonight?"

Sophia blinked. Lucy and Arabella looked expectant. "I beg your pardon?"

Lucy rolled her eyes, as was her wont. "This charity ball Lady Romeril is hosting—I never thought you went much in for that sort of thing."

"I have always been interested in charity," Sophia said defensively.

Her cheeks betrayed her, even if her words did not. It was not a complete lie. All the Fitzroys gave to charity, but this…this was different.

A charity ball. Though Sophia had no idea who else was on the guestlist, Lady Romeril moved in impressive circles, and it was unthinkable the viscount had not received an invitation.

After all, he had said himself how interested he was in charity affairs.

He had to be there. And that meant, Sophia thought wildly, she would see him again tonight. A mere two weeks until Christmas, the cold growing ever more freezing, nothing could ice her scalding heart. The things he did to her…

"Who do you know is attending?" asked Arabella.

Sophia swallowed. She would not permit herself to flush…

"I do not," she said as airily as she could, reaching for her jade green earrings. Earrings that had become her favorite ever since she caught a glimpse of Orlando's green eyes.

Her earrings did not quite compare to them, but she could not help but be reminded of them as she fixed them in her ears. Just another hour, and she would surely see him…

"Well, I suppose we should be grateful you are still attending balls."

Sophia started, looking curiously at Lucy. "What do you mean by that?"

"Oh, just something Arabella said."

Sophia glared at Arabella, who had the good grace to look a little ashamed.

"I did not mean anything by it! I merely said you had asked about—"

"I really must be going," said Sophia hastily, rising to her feet and looking for her pelisse. "I would hate to be really late."

"Are not all the young ladies of the *ton* looking to be fashionably late these days?" asked Lucy, getting up from the bed.

Sophia tried not to laugh as she left her bedchamber and started down the stairs, followed by her sisters. "You say that as though you are no longer young anymore."

"Trust me, the moment you are married, you are no longer considered young by Society," Lucy said dryly. "Why, I was saying to Percy only the other day—"

"I really must be going," said Sophia quickly.

The last thing she needed was an inquisition about the questions she had posed to Mrs. Castle and Arabella—and if either of them had mentioned a thing to Lucy, there would no end of hearing about it.

"Good evening, Mama, Papa!"

The drawing room door opened to reveal both her parents.

"Going so soon?" asked her father.

"Sophia is in a *hurry*," said Lucy in that teasing way of hers.

Sophia did not permit herself to be caught in that trap. After kissing her mother swiftly on the cheek, she rushed out of the house and slammed the door behind her. The carriage was waiting. She would be there soon, would see him…

"Invitation?" the footman sneered, standing at the door of Lady Romeril's home.

Sophia tried to smile at the servant as she handed over her gilded invitation. *Really,* she thought, *Lady Romeril could have given far more to this charitable cause if she had just sent simple invitations and not gone wild with the gold gilt.* There must be three shillings' worth on there!

"Ah, Miss Fitzroy," said the footman, glancing at her invitation. "Welcome."

"Thank you," Sophia simpered.

One never know what report a servant may take back to their mistress, and she was not going to permit Lady Romeril to have an ill impression of her. The last thing she needed was to lose the good graces of one of the most preeminent ladies of Society.

The place was absolutely heaving. Sophia tried not to step on any toes as she pushed her way through the hall, which was packed with people exchanging greetings and carefully looking at each other's gowns, and tried to enter the large ballroom.

Here, at least, she could catch her breath and look around. Sophia's gaze flickered across the many gentlemen she could see—a few she recognized, chattering away, some with cigars, all with the decided disadvantage of not being Orlando.

Where was he? Surely a viscount would be invited to such an event…even if he did have the most terrible reputation.

Sophia's heart raced, but started to slow as realization dawned. He was not here.

It was not that she had only come here to see him, far from it…but she could not help but admit to herself that without him, the ball simply would not be as enjoyable.

"Looking for me?"

Sophia's heart soared. She knew that voice—knew it better

than perhaps she ought.

"Orlando," she said impulsively as she turned.

Orlando grinned broadly. "I thought you weren't going to call me that."

"I thought you didn't host charitable concerts and refuse to kiss young ladies when alone with them," Sophia said a little breathlessly. "But here we are."

Here we are indeed. She could barely think; all her senses were focused on the man before her—but thinking did not appear to be necessary. Not when feeling was possible.

Orlando took her hand and kissed it. Sophia felt his lips press against her hands like a brand...as though she was marked forever as his own. As though no other man would now ever touch her, because *he* had touched her.

"You were looking for me, then?" he asked softly.

Sophia pulled her hand away, returning it to her side as the sensation of his lips continued to burn her skin. "Absolutely not."

A wide grin crossed his face. "Good, because I was hoping you were not here."

"You are—"

"Charming? Effervescent?"

"Most infuriating," Sophia admitted weakly.

Oh, how did he manage to do that to her? Though the ballroom was crowded with Lady Romeril's guests, all had faded away so that the only person in the room she could truly focus on was him.

Standing with a strange sort of lazy elegance, Orlando looked entirely at home in the place, as though he frequently attended balls. Sophia was sure their paths must have crossed before, albeit briefly...so how was it possible she had never noticed him before?

"Infuriating?" Orlando raised an eyebrow, and Sophia felt that throbbing between her legs again. "I do not believe I have ever been so insulted in my life."

"Yet you enjoyed it," Sophia found herself saying, stepping toward him, instincts now taking over, unable to think, merely to feel, knowing just how she longed to be close to him.

His green eyes caught hers, and his mouth opened with a teasing smile—then Orlando grabbed Sophia's wrist and jerked her toward him.

"Orlando!"

It was small relief that Sophia did not yelp his name loudly enough to disgrace herself—which would have been the outcome if anyone at Lady Romeril's ball had heard her speak so intimately to such a man.

But she could not think of that now. The viscount had not, as she had first thought, pulled her into his arms for an embrace, but was instead pulling her out of the ballroom, hurriedly down a corridor, and into a dark room.

"Orlando! What are you—"

"Shush!"

Sophia tried to catch her breath as she stood staring at the gentleman who had just released her and was now crouching by the door, an ear to it, listening closely. He was pale, as though he had seen something that had given him a remarkable fright.

It was most unaccountable.

"Orlando, why did you—"

"Shush!"

As she was not apparently going to be given any reason as to why they had suddenly vacated the ballroom and disappeared into a dark room, Sophia looked around.

They were in a library. Bookshelves lined the walls, their gold-embossed titles unreadable in the gloom, though her eyes were starting to adjust. It was colder in here after the crush of bodies warming Lady Romeril's ballroom, but that was not the reason why the hairs on her arms were standing up.

She was alone, once again, with Orlando—and this time, she knew what she wanted. What she would not leave this room without.

"You look most shaken," said Sophia in a low voice, still unsure why they were hiding. She approached Orlando, touching his shoulder gingerly as though he would burst into flames if she made contact. "Are you quite well?"

"I think so," breathed Orlando, glancing over his shoulder with a smile. "Yes, I think so."

"Whom are we hiding from?"

He took a deep breath as he turned around, and paced past her to a bookshelf. He was looking at the books when he said quietly, "Lady Romeril is out there."

"Of course she is," said Sophia with a frown. "It is her ball."

Orlando groaned, eyes closing for a moment before affixing on her once more. "I knew I should not have come."

It was impossible to prevent shock from searing across Sophia's chest. No, she must be mistaken; it was not possible for the assumption that had appeared in her mind to be true.

Viscount Orlando Dunbar...and Lady Romeril...

"You haven't bedded Lady Romeril!" she blurted out, coming toward him and looking Orlando directly in the eyes.

Orlando grinned. "A gentleman never tells."

Sophia's jaw fell open. Well, really—this was too far. More scandalous than she could ever have predicted! How had a man such as him... Well, that was not the question, was it?

She could well see how any woman would eventually cave in to the designs of a gentleman like Orlando.

But Lady Romeril!

He was laughing. "How your mind does wander, Sophia. Never let me underestimate you again. No, Lady Romeril and I have not had that particular...pleasure. But Lady Rose, on the other hand..."

Sophia's cheeks flushed. "Lady Romeril's daughter?"

Orlando inclined his head. "The very same. A delectable woman."

It was all she could do not to turn in embarrassment and leave the room this instant. Yes, Sophia knew Orlando had seduced many ladies, but that was easy to accept in the abstract.

But actually having one of those ladies mentioned to her, by name…

Sophia did turn away, unsure what Orlando would read in her eyes. "I see."

Desperate to distract herself from the very male presence of Orlando in the seemingly small room, Sophia walked to another wall and ran her fingers lightly across the spines of the books.

What had she got herself into?

"So if you do not mind, I would rather stay out of Lady Romeril's way for a little while," said Orlando lightly, as though he admitted to bedding daughters of noblemen all the time. "Best to stay out of sight."

Sophia swallowed. This gentleman…why, he could suggest to her that they steal the moon and she would follow him. How did he have this effect on her—an effect that clearly worked with so many others?

It was this last thought that spurred her on to speak again.

"You do not think that your future wife might…might be upset that you have bedded so many people?"

Sophia turned as she spoke, and gasped to find Orlando mere inches from her. He must have walked across the room silently, and was now so close her chest was pressed up against his.

Orlando took a step forward, his green eyes fixed on her, and Sophia was forced to step backward also, her back now touching the bookshelf. There was nowhere else to go—and it would be impossible to escape him as his hands reached up either side of her to pin her in place.

"Why?" Orlando breathed. "Are you applying for the position?"

Sophia swallowed, heart racing, desperate to feel his touch, to be closer, even closer than they were. Was that her pulse she could feel echoing through her body, or his own, his chest close to hers?

"Absolutely not," she replied.

"Good," said Orlando. "Then you won't mind if I do this."

His lips crushed against hers so suddenly, so powerfully, that

Sophia immediately raised her hands against his chest protective-ly—but then tightened them around his coat to pull him closer as the pleasure of his kiss overwhelmed her.

For a first kiss, this was certainly not what she had expected. It was better. Tingles of pleasure rippled through her body, undulating through her curves, and Sophia gasped, unable to bear it, overwhelmed by the hedonistic pleasure.

And then she moaned.

Orlando's tongue teased along her lips, demanding entry, and she let him in.

How could she do anything else? The man was a master, knowing precisely how she wanted to be kissed, how every twist and turn of his tongue would shatter her, make all thought unnecessary.

His hands had moved, and though Sophia's eyes were closed with the intensity of the pleasure, she felt the scalding heat of his touch on her waist.

"Sophia…"

His fingers tightened, and Sophia moaned again, moving her hands from his chest to the nape of his neck, pulling Orlando closer. She had to have him closer, had to have more of him. Precisely what that looked like, she could not tell.

The kiss ended, and Sophia gazed lustfully up into Orlando's dark eyes.

"You taste even better than you look," he growled.

"You kiss even better than you talk," Sophia whispered, pull-ing him closer again.

This time the kiss was less urgent, less hurried, and she melt-ed into his arms as he nibbled her lips, sending pleasure soaring through her.

This was…this was more than she could have ever imagined. More than she could have hoped for.

Giving herself up to the sensual delights Orlando was creating within her, Sophia closed her eyes once more as his kisses trailed down her neck, causing shivers down her spine, as his hands moved from her waist and started to pull down her gown from her shoulders—

"Stop."

Orlando broke the kiss, looking down at her with eyes hazed with desire. "Sophia?"

Sophia tried to breathe, tried to remember what it was to think. Goodness, she could kiss that man from now until kingdom come, but there were lines, and she had discovered one.

"I-I am not one of your French hens," she managed to say, gazing into his eyes.

Orlando swallowed, removed his hands from her, and raised them in mock surrender. "I submit."

Why precisely did those words spark desire in her? Sophia tried to push it to the side, her shoulders shuddering as she tried to calm her breathing.

"I...I think we should return to the ball," Sophia said.

Orlando shrugged, stepping backward to leave her escape clear. "There you go."

Sophia had stepped to the door and placed her hand on the handle before she realized that he was not following her. "Are...are you not coming with me?"

He shook his head.

"Because...because you still wish to avoid Lady Romeril?" Sophia asked.

A wry sort of smile crept over Orlando's face as he stepped backward again and sank into an armchair. "Because you have started something within me, Miss Sophia Fitzroy, and I need to finish it."

Sophia dropped her gaze to his breeches, saw the hardness of his manhood, and flushed.

"So while you are out there, dancing the night away," said Orlando in a low voice, fingers reaching for his breeches, "I will be here, thinking of you, pleasuring myself."

Sophia wrenched open the door, stepped through it, and slammed it.

She leaned against it, hoping the wood would cool her—but it did no such thing. Quite to the contrary, she could now hear what was happening in the library behind her.

"Sophia," moaned Orlando jaggedly, breath heaving. "Sophia…"

Knowing she should move, knowing she should certainly not be hearing such a thing, Sophia did not stir an inch. She stood there, heart pounding, the throbbing between her legs quickening its pace as she listened to the Viscount Dunbar pleasure himself to ecstasy at the mere thought of her.

CHAPTER SIX

A CHRISTMAS CAROL was being sung as Sophia entered Hyde Park.

She shivered. A chilly December wind rustled by her, but it did not encourage her to return home. Home was full of noise, excited chatter about the visit to Chalcroft they would be making for Christmas Day, preparations and wrapping and questions about Lady Romeril's ball…

And that was the last thing Sophia needed.

She needed to clear her head. *Think.* Actually try to understand what on earth was happening.

Because whatever had happened last night, and she was still attempting to understand just what that had been, she could not understand it.

"So while you are out there, dancing the night away, I will be here, thinking of you, pleasuring myself."

Sophia swallowed as she walked past a pair of ladies sitting on a bench, chattering away, her cheeks flushing at the scandalous memory that soared through her mind.

She should not have stayed to listen—and yet she had never felt more alive.

She had…not precisely controlled him, but certainly affected him in a way she could never have predicted. While Orlando certainly had an effect on her, it was nothing, it seemed, compared to the effect she had on him.

Which did not make sense. True, Sophia had wished for a romance—a scandalous romance, if she recalled correctly from her conversation with Caroline at Almack's—but that did not mean she was willing to lose her reputation.

And to a man like Orlando…

"How your mind does wander, Sophia. Never let me underestimate you again. No, Lady Romeril and I have not had that particular…pleasure. But Lady Rose, on the other hand…"

"Lady Romeril's daughter?"

"The very same. A delectable woman."

Sophia gritted her teeth. No, there was a man who saw no issue with taking a lady's innocence and leaving them by the wayside, literally hiding in libraries to avoid them.

That was not a gentleman with whom she should be associating.

So why was it that she was so drawn to him?

"You are just being foolish," Sophia told herself quietly, as the path before her was empty for a good twenty yards. "Making a fool of yourself, more like."

For was that not what she was doing? Was she not making it abundantly clear to all those around her, even if she thought she was being clever, that she was…

Falling in love?

Sophia swallowed and tried to push the thought from her mind. She was not falling in love; she had only met Orlando a few weeks ago! She was not about to throw away her reputation, her place in the Fitzroy family, for a viscount who did not know what was due her!

"You do not think that your future wife might…might be upset that you have bedded so many people?"

"Why? Are you applying for the position?"

"Absolutely not."

He had been teasing, of course. No rake like that would ever wish to marry her—in her rather limited experience, no rake wished to marry at all. It was simply beyond their purview; they were interested in bedding, not wedding.

No, she had come here to clear her head, and the best way to do that, as the sound of the Christmas carol "The First Noel" grew louder, was to ignore Orlando completely.

Which would be a great deal easier if he had not just walked into the park.

Sophia's heart leapt most traitorously. Goodness, if she could not even stop herself from feeling joy at the mere sight of him, what was she to do?

Was she truly falling in love with him? How was that possible?

Try as she might, Sophia could not stop looking at Orlando as he took the path she was on, but from the other direction. He was so handsome, so tall—so utterly charming. The way he kissed... Sophia had not even believed it possible to stir such emotions.

Yet he had. Oh, he had, and she wanted them to be stirred again. Wanted more. Wanted all he could give her.

But this was ridiculous—she could not talk to Orlando in public! Who knew what he would say?

A wry smile crept across her face, despite herself. She knew very well the sort of things he would say, which was precisely why she should be avoiding him at all costs. Yet her feet, inexplicably, continued her down the path as Sophia's heart started to beat faster, her fingers tingling in anticipation.

And then he saw her. His eyes, green even from this distance, caught hers, and a lurch most unbecoming of a young lady soared through her stomach.

Sophia swallowed. Oh, she was in danger. It had been her sister Esther, hadn't it, who fell in love with a duke in just a matter of weeks? Was she about to fall into the same trap...but with a viscount who had absolutely no intention of marrying her?

She hardly knew him! Yet there was something about him, something Sophia could not describe. Something that made her absolutely certain she had to be with him. Be close to him. Whatever else happened…

Was it just her imagination, or did Orlando look nervous to see her?

"Miss Fitzroy," he said formally, bowing his head to her as they met.

Sophia halted, heart still beating frantically as she stood before him and dipped into a low curtsey. When she raised her head, there was that sardonic smile she knew so well.

She must have been imagining the nerves she had thought she spied on his face. Orlando Dunbar, nervous? Nonsense.

"My lord," said Sophia, mischief seeping into her voice. "So formal, my goodness. Does that mean you have decided to be a gentleman and treat me like a lady?"

"I have certainly treated you like a lady already in our acquaintance, I assure you," came the teasing reply. "Would you like me to treat you otherwise? Like a lady of the street, perhaps?"

Sophia shivered, hoping to goodness Orlando did not see the very physical reaction she had to his words. A lady of the street, indeed! It was an outrage, even suggesting to compare her to such a woman!

And yet from his lips…from his lips it felt more an invitation. One she could not refuse. One she did not wish to refuse.

Images flooded her mind, some Sophia did not even truly understand, but her imagination went wild, showing her a vision of her and Orlando, their bodies entirely naked, entwined on a bed as moans of ecstasy rose into the air…

"Sophia?"

"Yes? Yes," said Sophia hurriedly.

There must have been a glazed expression on her face, or she had not responded to something that Orlando had said, for he was looking at her most curiously.

Or perhaps that was just her imagination. *I must not permit my imagination to get the better of me*, Sophia told herself sternly, highly conscious of a few gentlemen walking past them, one giving herself and Orlando a curious glance.

She was speaking in public with the Viscount Dunbar.

"I said, are you going for a walk anywhere in particular?" repeated Orlando with a teasing smile. "Goodness, one would almost think you were…distracted by someone."

"Something," said Sophia hastily.

Lord, the last thing she needed was for Orlando to realize just what an effect he had on her! If he did not already know…

"You taste even better than you look."

"You kiss even better than you talk."

"Indeed?" Orlando said, indicating the path with his hand.

Sophia hesitated only for a moment. *What harm can a walk do?* They were in public, after all, and it was not as though Orlando was likely to kiss her while in the park.

Even if she may wish him to…

"Sophia?"

"What?" she said distractedly. "Yes, right. Walking."

Did she have to sound such a fool? Sophia cringed as she stepped forward along the path, Orlando beside her, and tried to get her mind in order.

She was going for a walk—an unchaperoned walk!—with the Viscount Dunbar. If anyone saw her, her mother would know about it before she even got home.

That meant she had to at least be able to say, truthfully, there was nothing untoward in their conversation. And that meant sticking to topics that could not be misrepresented as…well, seduction.

Heat tinged her cheeks, despite the coldness of the afternoon. *Just talk!*

"Yes, I was thinking of my family's plans for this Christmas," Sophia said airily.

How was it Caroline spoke with confidence that no one could possibly say anything more interesting than her, everything she said was perfect, no word could be improved?

How did she *do* that?

Orlando nodded as he walked alongside her. "Christmas plans. Indeed."

"We are going to Chalcroft this year, something I admit I am excited about," said Sophia, not able to dampen her enthusiasm.

Chalcroft. Her father was the youngest of three, and her eldest uncle lived at the family seat, Chalcroft. Just outside Bath and usually in a terrible state of repair—at least, that was what her aunt Leonora always said—it was still the home of the Fitzroy family, and where they gathered almost every Christmas.

"Chalcroft?"

"The Fitzroy seat," said Sophia with a grin. "I know, 'tis probably nothing to the seat of a viscount—"

"I would not be so sure about that," said Orlando with a dry laugh. "Most of the Dunbar property was frittered away by my brother, the previous viscount."

Curiosity curled around Sophia's heart. Now, finally, she was starting to get a little insight into the mysterious Viscount Dunbar.

"Oh?"

"Do not give me that, Sophia. I think we know each other…well enough, shall we say, for you to ask me a question outright," Orlando said, eyebrow rising.

Sophia tried her best not to flush, but it was rather difficult not to. It was the closest comment about their passionate kissing only last evening, something she had promised herself she would not mention. But as he had invited her to ask questions…

"Well, what happened to him?"

"Killed in a duel," said Orlando matter-of-factly, as though one's siblings were killed in duels all the time. "Fool."

Sophia stared at the man beside her. "I beg your pardon?"

"The most important thing to consider when deflowering princesses," said Orlando in an undertone as a matronly looking woman passed, "is to make sure fathers are not in Town."

Heat scalded Sophia's cheeks as she looked away, trying to find the trees lining the path remarkably interesting. How could he say such a thing—deflowering princesses, indeed!

If it had been anyone else, she would have said they were attempting to impress her merely by spouting nonsense, but with Orlando…

Sophia's heart contracted painfully for a moment. This was a man with whom she should not be flirting. Or even conversing.

"So you were quite alike, then?" She tried to say it archly.

Orlando glanced at her and grinned. "Completely different."

Hope soared in her chest. Perhaps the gossip about Orlando was entirely mistaken. He had kissed her, certainly, and bedded Lady Romeril's daughter…but if that was all…

"Well, you know what they say. You cannot always believe the rumors."

"Yes, I would always ensure both fathers and brothers were well away before deflowering anyone," Orlando continued.

Sophia's shoulders slumped. Of course he did. When would she learn she was just another one of the many ladies with whom he was flirting? Definitely not the most impressive, either. She had no title—a fine dowry, yes, but nothing to tempt a man who seduced *princesses*!

"You look disappointed."

Sophia took a deep breath. "I suppose I am."

As she glanced over at Orlando, it was to see a rather strange expression on his face. Was that…disappointment of his own?

"After all," she continued, trying to inject mirth into her voice, "you made a mistake, did you not? You may have chased away fathers and brothers, but I think it is the mothers you should look out for—and I think Lady Romeril would agree!"

Orlando's laughter echoed around the park, and Sophia's heart leapt for joy. She had made him do that; she had put the smile on his face, made him chuckle most heartily. Her words, her cleverness…

And if you think that's enough to capture his heart, she told herself sternly, *you are very much mistaken.* Orlando Dunbar did not fall in love with ladies who could make him laugh. As far as she could tell, Orlando Dunbar did not fall in love at all.

"Well said," admitted Orlando with a shake of his head.

"I suppose," Sophia said, unable to prevent herself from speaking openly as they turned a corner on the path, "I am the only one you are kissing in libraries at the moment."

The words hung in the air, unable to be taken back, but Sophia did not wish to. Perhaps it was time to be bold—as she was sure Orlando's three French hens were. They probably did not wait around for him to visit them; they took the initiative and went to find him.

Well, this was her moment to take the initiative…even if it did make her stomach nauseated and her fingers tingle…

"What an interesting question," said Orlando quietly. "What makes you think you are the only one?"

Sophia's heart skipped a beat. She needed to leave, walk away from this teasing, delicious man, and prevent herself from even considering falling under his charms again.

Orlando Dunbar knew precisely what a lady wanted, and that was all the more reason to make sure he never gave it to her.

"I see," she said coldly. "Well, good day, my lord. I hope you enjoy your—"

"Wait."

Sophia had only just turned, not even taken a step away, when Orlando took her hand.

She froze, utterly transfixed. They had halted on the path; others were around them, but she was not paying any attention to them. How could she? Her gaze was affixed on a green stare. What could Orlando want with her—and why was he holding so tightly to her fingers?

"Sophia Fitzroy, you minx," he murmured, stepping toward her and not releasing her hand. "You were actually going to walk away from me, weren't you?"

Sophia tried to take a breath. "Are you unaccustomed to ladies deciding to leave you?"

"Very much so," he said quietly. "And I find I do not like it at all."

"Well then, you know how to avoid it." Was she brave enough to say this? It appeared her tongue had a mind of its own, in any case. "Stop kissing other ladies."

"I can't."

"Well then—"

"Wait!" Orlando held tightly to her hand as Sophia made to pull it away, and there was a desperate look on his face she had never seen before. "I cannot stop kissing other ladies because…because…"

Sophia stared up at him. What was so difficult to say? What was Orlando unwilling to admit to her?

"Because," he said softly, now only a murmur, "I am not kissing any other ladies."

Sophia stared. He could not be earnest. He could not be! Everything she had heard of the handsome, charming, debonair Viscount Dunbar told her he was undoubtedly kissing many a lady under mistletoe this Christmas, and in other places the rest of the year.

But there was such an odd look on his face…she could almost believe him.

"You are teasing me."

Orlando pulled her toward him. "I am not. Sophia Fitzroy, you have pushed every other woman quite forcibly out of my mind, and I…I don't know what to do about it."

Sophia swallowed. She had stopped Orlando from…from kissing other ladies? How on earth could that be?

"In that case," she said, unable to look elsewhere and certain they were attracting attention standing in this way, "why not court me? Officially, I mean, speak to my father?"

"Because that would take all the fun out of it."

Sophia's heart leapt. She could not help it. She had tried to force down all her hopes, all expectations, but it was impossible.

Take all the fun out of it… What could he possibly mean, other than he intended to bed her? That those kisses, those searing kisses she could not stop thinking about, were only a prelude to something much deeper, much darker? Surely that meant...

"Ah, Orlando!"

Sophia jerked her hand away from Orlando's as a woman she did not recognize approached them, beaming at the viscount.

"I thought I would find you here. This is always the best place to find young ladies in need of a little flattery," said the woman breezily, smiling thinly at Sophia before turning back to Orlando. "We had a rendezvous organized yesterday, and you, my man, did not meet it!"

"Ah," said Orlando weakly, not looking at Sophia, who remained by his side. "Miss Tilbury..."

Sophia could not breathe. She could feel her chest tighten, unmoving, as she watched the dazzling conversation before her: the known seductress and the known seducer, organizing another opportunity to...to...

Well. She knew precisely what. They did not need to say it.

Disappointment rushed through her, bitter and cold, dampening all the hope and excitement that had been sparked by Orlando's words.

He'd had a rendezvous with Miss Tilbury just yesterday, had he? So that was perhaps why he was so...so fired up. Sophia could think of no other way to describe it. It was not merely her, her kisses, her embrace—it was the thought of Miss Tilbury to come.

"—when you will next—"

"I am so sorry, Miss Tilbury," cut in Orlando, and Sophia tried to focus as he spoke. "I regret to inform you I am no longer available for such...such meetings."

Sophia glanced at the woman. Miss Tilbury's nostrils flared, and she glanced just once at Sophia before laughing merrily.

"Ah, well, no matter. You were not my favorite encounter in any case," she said prettily, as though gentlemen rejected her in public all the time. "Do give my best to your brother, won't you?"

She wandered away without another word.

"Sophia—"

"Brother?" Sophia said, arching an eyebrow. Well, she had been put in her place and no mistake, even if Miss Tilbury had not spoken a word to her. "How interesting."

"No, Sophia—"

But Sophia did not wait to hear his excuses. Turning away, she started to walk hastily toward the gate to the park. She wanted to go home.

"Sophia, wait!"

Though she had no intention of waiting, it was rather difficult to shake him off—particularly when the viscount grabbed her shoulder and twisted her around.

"Get your hands off me!"

"Not until you hear me out," said Orlando darkly. "Sophia, I have three brothers!"

Sophia glared, unwilling to believe him, yet so desperate for him to be speaking the truth that she could not help but say, "Three?"

The viscount nodded. "You have five sisters; I have three brothers—and a sister, but that does not matter. One brother died in a duel, as I said, but at least one of the others, I believe, is about to become the keeper of Miss Tilbury. You must believe me."

Sophia hesitated. *I must believe him…* Well, it was all too easy to, when she wanted to so badly.

"You…you are a popular man," she said tentatively.

Orlando laughed dryly. "I would not call a close acquaintance with Miss Tilbury popular but…no, I know what you mean. I am popular, Sophia, because I know what a lady wants, and I give it to her. But I told you before. There is no one else receiving my…my attentions at the moment. Only you."

A shiver rushed down Sophia's spine. Could she believe him? Could she trust him? "But for Miss Tilbury to approach you and—and offer herself to you. You are popular indeed."

Orlando's hand drifted from her shoulder to her face, cupping her cheek in a way that made Sophia's cheeks flush. "Not with the woman who really counts."

CHAPTER SEVEN

"—AND I STILL say we should have Christmas here!"

Sophia sighed. Family arguments were likely to erupt this time of year, she knew that; too many Fitzroys in one place, and this was the result. But this had to be the most foolish argument she had ever heard.

"I thought we were agreed, months ago," she said wearily across the dinner table. "We are going to Chalcroft for Christmas!"

Almost every eye turned to her with a glare, and Sophia raised her hands in mock surrender. She had told herself not to get involved in the debate, and she had been right to.

It had been raging ever since the family sat down to dinner, one week before Christmas. Sophia had looked forward to having everyone together in one place. Now she was not so sure. Jemima had made the mistake of remarking how snow was in the air, and this had led to a debate.

Of course it had.

"Chalcroft may be entirely unreachable if snow does come!" Caroline pointed out, waving a fork with chicken on the end at Sophia. "And then what will we do?"

"We could always have Christmas here, like we did in the old days," said Arthur mildly, as though it was perfectly normal for his wife and six daughters—plus husbands—to argue over the dinner table. "Goodness, it has been years since we were all together…"

"Six years, I think," Esther said. "And isn't that what is most important? Being together?"

Sophia stifled a grin. Trust Esther to attempt peacekeeping. That was always her way, even in situations like this, when the entire conversation was redundant.

She wasn't even sure whether it would snow.

"Oh, it would be lovely to have you all here, with the grandchildren," said their mother with a beaming smile.

Sophia glanced nervously at Jemima. She had not forgotten the sudden and shocking tears Jemima had shed just two Christmases ago, when their cousin Harmony announced she was with child.

Despite being married six years now, Jemima and her husband Hugh had welcomed no child to their family. It was a sore topic, one they all avoided.

But Jemima did not look up. She was picking at her food, moving her roast chicken about her plate, and Sophia breathed a quiet sigh of relief. The last thing she wanted was for an outburst from perhaps the most fiery of the Fitzroy sisters.

"That's all very well, but I am not sure here will be large enough for all of us," pointed out Esther before she took a sip of wine. "After all, five of us are married, and with seven grandchildren—"

"You are about to suggest your townhouse, aren't you?" snapped Caroline.

Esther shrugged. "Well, it is the largest of all our London residences, and—"

"Just because you are a duchess, that does not make you the eldest!"

Sophia sighed and ate another mouthful of the delicious dinner. It was always the way with her sisters: they were perfectly pleasant in small doses, even in small numbers…

But bring all six together, as her parents had done this evening, and this was the result.

Mutinous faces glared at each other over the dining table.

Their father cleared his throat. "Well, as we do not know whether or not we can attend Chalcroft—"

"But if we cannot, we must have a plan," said Lucy with a mischievous grin. "Do not you think, Arabella?"

Arabella, seemingly startled to be brought into the debate, did nothing but stick her tongue out at her teasing sister.

Sophia chuckled. Trust Bels not to be foolish enough to be tricked by Lucy into the argument.

"Well, I still think Kendal House is the best suited to host Christmas," Esther said, smiling weakly at Caroline in an attempt to make her smile likewise.

The Countess of Cheshire, as Caroline's title was now, did not smile. "You hosted Easter. I think it most unfair…"

Sophia sipped her wine and carefully halved a roast potato before popping it into her mouth. She had little interest in sparking more fury from one or more of her sisters, and besides, her mind was entirely taken up with far more pleasant matters.

"You are popular indeed."

"Not with the woman who really counts."

A little shiver rushed through her, and she tried to focus on her plate rather than the sensuous delights silently promised in those words from Orlando just two days ago.

They had continued to walk after that. How could she leave him? How could she walk away from him knowing—at least, trusting—that she was the one person in the whole of London that he wished to be with?

It still did not feel entirely real, and Sophia was attempting not to permit her mind to believe every word he said.

After all, she was right. Why not court her properly, if she was really overtaking his mind like that?

Because, a cruel little voice whispered in her ear, *you are not entirely sure, are you? Is Orlando Dunbar, a viscount known for seducing women far prettier and far more impressive than you, a man to be trusted?*

And Sophia knew the answer: that she should not be seriously considering the viscount as a suitor—or a seducer. The last thing she needed was for such a man to...to get under her skin. To touch her skin as he had done in that library.

Sophia swallowed and looked down at her plate, rather astonished to find it empty. She could not recall eating the last few mouthfuls of her meal.

"—don't you think, Sophia?"

She looked up hurriedly to see the entire table staring at her. "What?"

Lucy giggled. "You really must pay attention, Sophia—what on earth is distracting you from such an important discussion?"

Esther nudged her, frowning at her levity, and Lucy giggled again.

Sophia smiled weakly. "Oh, nothing."

"Nothing?" Caroline raised an eyebrow. "So the reports I have heard of you speaking with and walking with a *certain gentleman* are not preoccupying your mind?"

A burning flush rushed across Sophia's cheeks as mouths fell open up and down the table. What did Caroline think she was doing, speaking such nonsense before her sisters like that—before their parents!

The fact it was true was completely beside the point...

Sophia attempted to sit up a little straighter, as though she had nothing to be ashamed of. And she didn't—at least, as far as Caroline knew. All her sister had been told, clearly, was that Sophia and the Viscount Dunbar had walked in the park.

She could not know about their encounter in the library...

"A certain gentleman?" repeated their mother, eyebrow raised. "Goodness, Sophia, you do surprise me!"

"You don't surprise me," said Lucy with a wicked grin. "Come on, then, out with it. Who is it?"

"No one," Sophia said automatically.

It did not appear a single member of her family was going to be convinced.

"Sophia Fitzroy, you little liar!" That was Caroline.

Jemima was grinning, though she looked a little pale. "I never would have had you down as the rebellious one, Soph!"

"Who is it?" asked Arabella, looking between Sophia and Caroline. "And why did you call him a *certain gentleman?*"

"There is nothing to talk about," said Sophia desperately. The last thing she wished was for her family to truly think that there was something in her sister's words!

Orlando was…private. Hers, and hers alone. At least, until she could ascertain whether he was truly interested in her, or—

"Tell me right now, or I shall scream," pronounced Lucy matter-of-factly. "I need to know who it is!"

"There is nothing to tell," Sophia insisted, heart pounding now as she faced the curiosity and ire of her family. "There is no certain gentle—"

"The Viscount Dunbar," said Mrs. Castle, their housekeeper, by the door.

Every single Fitzroy head turned. Sophia could barely believe this was happening—it was surely a dream, or a nightmare, was it not?

But as she slowly turned in her seat to look at the door, she saw standing there a tall, handsome man with green eyes and a wicked grin on his face. He was looking directly at her.

"Viscount Dunbar?" repeated her papa slowly.

"The Viscount Dunbar," said Caroline in a satisfied voice.

Arabella looked at the gentleman before them, then turned to Sophia and hissed, "The Viscount Dunbar?"

"Good evening," said Orlando. "Yes, the Viscount Dunbar. Hello."

Sophia almost slipped off her chair, she was so mortified. What was he doing here? What did he think he was doing, arriving at this time of the evening—it was dinnertime to any civilized person!

But, of course, that was the point, wasn't it? Orlando was not civilized, and he was certainly not looking at her in a civilized manner.

Heat poured through her chest. Did he have to…well, look at her as though he would quite like to eat her?

Whispers were rustling through the room, and Sophia attempted not to pick out words and phrases from her sisters, but it was impossible.

"A *certain* gentleman?"

"Surely not."

"Not our Sophia…"

"—and him?"

"Mr. Fitzroy," said Orlando, bowing to the man at the head of the table.

Sophia twisted and watched her father incline his head to the stranger who had so rudely stepped into their dining room. How could she escape this nightmare without offending either her father, or the gentleman who was fast becoming more important to her than anyone?

"My *lord*," she said, turning to Orlando and wishing her sisters were not all there. "You are mistaken in thinking you can come here and—"

"I wish to formally ask your permission, Mr. Fitzroy, to court your daughter," said Orlando grandly.

Sophia's heart skipped a beat painfully as excitement rushed through her.

He could not be serious. What did Orlando think he was doing? Did he not know his own reputation, not know what this would look like? What father would ever permit—

"Court my daughter?" repeated Arthur.

Sophia tried to look at her father, but there was such astonishment on his face that she had to look away—her gaze was pulled inexorably back to the gentleman who had caused such a stir by his entrance and strange pronouncement.

"Court Sophia?" said her mother breathlessly.

Sophia knew her cheeks were pinking, knew it would be

impossible to make her parents calm, but she had to stop this nonsense. Orlando was just teasing, surely, but this was not a joke that any of the Fitzroys would understand!

Why, they may actually think him serious!

"Orlan—Viscount Dunbar," she hissed. "What are you—"

"After a pleasant walk with your daughter at Hyde Park, she pointed out to me how very remiss I had been in not requesting your permission to court her," said Orlando with a grin. "And so, of course, once I had completed a little…business, I decided to rectify that mistake immediately."

This was too much. Sophia stood up hurriedly, and her napkin fell to the floor as her sisters gasped.

"Come with me," she said sternly to the gentleman grinning broadly. "Now."

"Sophia—"

"Where are you going?"

Her parents' questions were roundly ignored. Grabbing Orlando's sleeve and trying not to think what her entire family must be thinking after that ridiculous speech, Sophia pulled the viscount out into the hall and slammed the door to the dining room behind her.

"Just what," she said darkly, "do you think you are doing?"

"My word, Miss Sophia Fitzroy, you do know how to glare at a gentleman," said Orlando in a low voice, as an explosion of voices burst out through the door beside them.

Sophia tried her best to take a deep, long, calming breath. What had happened?

Orlando had appeared at her home, astonishing her family and confirming—certainly in Caroline's mind—precisely whatever it was Sophia had been accused of. Orlando had made some…some idiotic speech about courting her, then said that she had demanded he do such a thing. And now she had dragged him out into the hall away from her family, surely confirming to them precisely what she did not wish them to think.

Sophia sagged against the wall. *Oh, what a tangle. What a mess.*

"You know, you do not look half as excited as I thought you would, having me declare my intentions to your family."

Sophia looked up at Orlando, who had a rakish grin across his face. He was…he was enjoying this! He thought it amusing! *Well, two can play at that game…*

"I am just concerned, that is all," she said as airily as she could manage, trying to ignore the excitement rushing through her veins.

Was it possible that he could be serious? Was the rake, the scoundrel Viscount Dunbar actually serious about courting her, about…marrying her?

Orlando's smile flickered. "Concerned?"

"Well, what about your rakish reputation?" Sophia said in a teasing voice, watching him closely. "Is that not in jeopardy now you have announced yourself as my suitor?"

"Perhaps," said Orlando with a grin, "but what use is my rakish reputation to me now? I am willing to lose it…for you."

Sophia's smile disappeared. He was rather too good at flirting, she had to admit…but there was a depth to it now that had not been there before. A depth she did not understand.

He could not be truly growing affection for her…could he? Attraction, yes, she could well believe it after their encounter in the library.

But true, genuine affection?

"You are not serious," she breathed.

"Never more so."

"But…but what about your three French hens?"

"Oh, them," said Orlando dismissively, waving a gloved hand. "What about them?"

Emboldened by she knew not what, Sophia stepped closer to him—so that she could whisper, she told herself sternly. For no other reason.

"I rather had the impression from Miss Tilbury that the ladies you bed would be disappointed to lose you," she said quietly.

Orlando's eyes flickered across her face. For a moment he

said nothing, merely examining her, as though she was a painting he had been bidden to memorize. A flicker of pleasure rushed through Sophia's body to be so close to him, to be his focus. Was this what every woman felt whenever they were close to him?

"They will find other men," he said softly, "but I will not find other Sophias."

Heat scalded Sophia's cheeks. He was teasing her, that was all; this was all one huge jest to him, she knew it!

"You know, you run the risk of ruining my reputation just by coming here, Orlando," Sophia said quietly.

Oh, how she longed to reach out and take his hand. It was so close, ungloved despite the inclement December weather, that she could almost take it if she shifted ever so slightly…

Orlando grinned wickedly. "Excellent. I will start to bring you down to my level."

Sophia swallowed, unsure precisely what to say to such a pronouncement. What a cad he was! And yet a delicious cad, a delectable cad. A cad she wanted to know better, even though her better judgment was screaming that she should run, flee, disappear as quickly as she could from this gentleman who seemed determined to ruin her.

Oh, if he would ruin her…

"Well, you've made a complete fool of yourself, and me, by coming here and saying such nonsensical things," Sophia managed to say. "Now I think…I think you should leave."

Was that disappointment flitting across his face? Sophia could not tell—the hall was not as well lit as the dining room—but it was certainly not the charming and delightful Orlando she knew. What was going on?

"Fine, I will leave, if that is what you wish," said Orlando quietly. "But not without one last thing."

Before Sophia could do or say anything, he opened the dining room door. The loud chatter halted immediately.

"Mr. Fitzroy," Orlando said pleasantly. "May I borrow you for a moment?"

"Orlando," said Sophia, panic rushing through her veins, "what do you think you are—Hello, Papa."

Arthur looked between the two of them. "Hello."

"Somewhere private, if you do not mind, sir," said Orlando with a smile.

No, this absolutely cannot be happening, Sophia thought wildly. *Absolutely not!*

"His lordship can have nothing to say to you that he cannot say before me, I am sure," she said hastily, glaring at Orlando as best she could without her father seeing. "I would much rather—"

"My study is convenient, your lordship," said Papa stiffly.

Sophia watched in horror as the two men walked to the study and entered. Orlando shot her a grin as he closed the door. The hall fell silent.

She was not proud of what she did next, but what choice did she have? Moving as silently as she could, Sophia pressed her ear up against the door of her father's study and tried to slow her breathing enough to hear what was going on inside.

Muffled murmurs could be heard, but nothing else. It was just too thick a door, the words between her father and Orlando too soft, to make out what they were saying.

She could, however, hear footsteps.

Leaping away from the door and hoping neither of them heard her move, Sophia smiled weakly as the two men appeared again.

"What were you discuss—"

"Have a lovely evening, Sophia," said her father smartly. "I will see you tomorrow."

"Tomorrow?" repeated Sophia blankly. "But—"

"Come on, Miss Fitzroy," said Orlando with a wicked grin. "We are late."

CHAPTER EIGHT

THE COLD NIGHT air hit Sophia's lungs as she was pulled out of her home and into darkness.

"Orlando!"

But he paid her no heed. Heart thumping wildly, utterly at a loss to understand what was happening—and desperately wishing she'd had the presence of mind to grab a pelisse—Sophia saw a carriage standing outside the house with a crest upon it she did not recognize.

"There we are," said Orlando, pulling up by the door and opening it. "In you go."

Sophia stared up at the handsome man who at every turn was utterly confusing her. "You cannot be serious."

He grinned. "More serious than I have ever been in my life."

"B-but…it's the evening!" spluttered Sophia, glancing back at her home. Was that Lucy there, at the curtain, peering out at them? "Where are you taking me?"

"Somewhere that is not here."

"And where precisely might that be?" Sophia asked, shivering slightly as the December chill started to seep into her bones, mingling with the searing heat from her chest from a mere look at the viscount before her.

Orlando's smile softened, no longer the wicked, mischievous grin she knew so well, but something else. Something kinder, perhaps more real.

"Do you not want to come with me?"

Sophia hesitated, barely able to think in the whirlwind of Orlando's declaration to her family, strange private conversation with her father, and now this carriage ride…

Where was he hoping to take her? Did her father approve of this—was Orlando asking permission to take her on a carriage ride when he spoke to him in the study? But then why the secrecy, why the refusal to say what he was planning, where they were going?

It was all most unaccountable, and the trouble was, wild ideas were rushing through her mind that were far too distracting. Ideas such as kissing Orlando in the carriage, being taken to his home to be seduced…

"Well?"

Sophia swallowed. "But it… Orlando, it is pitch black out here! It's dark, it's night!"

"All the better," Orlando said in a low voice.

This was madness—the last thing she should do was get into the carriage of a known rake and disappear off into the night! Sophia knew it in the very fiber of her being: this was not the sort of thing that elegant, refined young ladies of the *ton* permitted to happen!

"Mr. Fitzroy. May I borrow you for a moment?"

But…if Orlando had already spoken with her father, told him what he intended, her father would not have permitted her to leave if he did not approve, surely? Was that not the best evidence that this was not the sordid suggestion it appeared?

Sophia looked into the dark green eyes of the man she was fast becoming devoted to.

How could she pass up this opportunity to…to whatever it was? If she retreated, returned the few steps home, would she not regret it for the rest of her life?

"Sophia Fitzroy," said Orlando softly. "When we first met, you said you wanted—"

"A scandalous romance, I remember," said Sophia with a laugh. "But I never expected—"

"And I never expected you," he said.

Without saying another word, Orlando stepped into the carriage. It rocked slightly, leaving Sophia standing alone by the door. What was she going to do?

"What I really want is a scandalous romance."

Sophia set her jaw, hitched up her skirts, and stepped into the carriage.

It was not the love nest she had supposed it to be. Oh, it was comfortable enough—there was a blanket there to keep the cold away, but nothing in particular that suggested this was where Orlando performed his…well, *seductions*.

Sophia pulled the carriage door, and its snap echoed with the beat of her heart. She had done it. She had got into the carriage of Orlando Dunbar, viscount, rake, scoundrel, cad, heartbreaker… Now what happened?

Orlando tapped the roof of the carriage, and it jerked forward. Sophia put out a hand to prevent herself from sliding across the seat, and wondered what on earth she had done.

"So," she said as lightly as she could manage, heart beating violently in her chest, "are you abducting me?"

Orlando chuckled. "Not quite."

"Not quite!"

"Well, I may have lied, just a little, to your father," the viscount said calmly. Sophia could make out, even in the gloom, that he was smiling. "I may have told him that I wished you to accompany me to dinner with some friends of mine. To introduce you to them."

Shock and confusion leached into Sophia's mind. "And instead we are…?"

The impression of a smile widened. "Don't worry, I'll feed you."

Sophia swallowed. There was something very predatory about the way Orlando was looking at her, as though it would be her on the menu.

"I cannot believe you lied to my father," she said.

She curled her fingers around the seat of the carriage as it rattled along the London streets. What did she think she was doing? She was perfectly aware Orlando was a rake, that he was not to be trusted—and now he'd just admitted, calmly and freely, that he had lied to her father.

Did that mean…her father had no idea where she was going?

"Do not worry about it," said Orlando quietly. "You'll eat. But not with others."

Sophia glanced at the window, but it was impossible to tell where they were. All London streets looked the same from a carriage at night, and from what she could see, it was starting to snow. She could be anywhere. Anywhere in London. If her family needed to come looking for her…where would they start?

"I can see your concern, even in the dark," came the amused voice of Orlando.

"I am not concerned."

"You don't lie nearly as well as me," he remarked.

Sophia glared in his general direction. "Good!"

"Sophia Fitzroy, what will I do with you?"

She shivered at those words. Filled with lust, desire, a recklessness that sparked across her body.

Even though it shouldn't. Sophia knew she should be repulsed, outraged by the way Orlando was acting…but it delighted and intrigued her more than was appropriate.

Nice young ladies did not get into carriages with lying rakes.

"Here we are."

Sophia glanced out of the window again as the carriage slowed then came to a gradual stop. The townhouse they had pulled up by was rather grand, though not as large as Esther's or Caroline's. Still, it appeared respectable—in stark contrast to her companion.

"Where are we?"

Orlando chuckled. "My home, of course."

Sophia's heart skipped a beat as Orlando reached past her and opened the carriage door. *His…his home?* She had been taken back to the viscount's home, in the dark of night, with no chaperone, against the wishes and without the knowledge of her father?

"Sophia?"

Sophia looked down at the hand protruding through the open carriage door and swallowed. She could demand to be taken home, of course. She could tell the driver right now to return her to the Fitzroy family home, and he may just do it.

But then…then she would miss out on whatever this was.

Whatever this experience with Orlando was, she would never know, never have the chance again to experience it, she was certain of that. She would regret missing it for the rest of her life.

Steeling herself as she imagined soldiers steeled themselves for battle, Sophia took Orlando's hand.

The hall was nondescript, but that was perhaps because it was so dark.

"Orlando?"

"Give me a moment," came the reply.

A spark of light, so dazzling Sophia had to hold up her hand to protect her eyes. Then it dimmed, warmed, and she could see Orlando had lit a candelabrum near the front door.

It was…well, a hall. If she had expected to unravel the secrets of the Viscount Dunbar merely by the decoration of his hall, Sophia was much mistaken. Three doors, a staircase, a coatrack, and an awfully ugly painting of a horse…and that was it.

A chuckle echoed. Sophia swept around to look at Orlando, who was grinning.

"What did you expect?" he said lightly. "Women lounging in every corner? My three French hens, perhaps, clucking for my return?"

Sophia's cheeks flushed. "No."

Yes. Perhaps? She had not been entirely sure what to expect, but it was not this, this…banality.

"The drawing room, I suppose, is in here," she said, stepping to a door.

She opened it, revealing a drawing room indeed, just as dull as the hallway. In the gloom she could make out a fireplace around which several armchairs and a sofa were arranged, a pianoforte in one corner and a grandfather clock in another.

But before she could look any further, a hand closed on hers.

"I am sure you would be very interested in looking all around my home," Orlando said sardonically, "but the room I would most like to show you is…up here."

A gentle tug on her hand twisted Sophia around so she was looking…up the staircase.

Sophia swallowed. Of course he did. Of course he wanted to take her upstairs—and there did not appear to be any servants up, either, to act as some sort of chaperone by accident.

No, they were alone here…and Orlando wanted to show her something upstairs.

"You…you are trying to seduce me, aren't you?"

Orlando answered in seemingly the only way he knew how: by kissing her.

Sophia gasped in his mouth as Orlando pushed her against the wall, his lips possessing hers so entirely that she had no choice but to give everything to him.

And she did not wish to hold anything back. Pleasure tingled down her spine as Orlando gently parted her lips with his own, and she gasped as his tongue teased hers.

Oh, this was everything she wanted, everything—a scandalous romance indeed! Kissing the Viscount Dunbar in his home, when no one else knew she was there… It was wonderful, and his hands on her waist made her feel weightless, as though she could soar up into the air…

The kiss ended as abruptly as it had begun. Sophia panted, hardly able to get her breath back, as she looked up into the dark green eyes of Orlando.

"Trying to seduce you?" he said with a jagged voice. "I'm not trying. I'm succeeding."

Sophia could not help but smile. Oh, he was amusing, witty, charming, caring—all the things she would wish for in a lover. And her parents thought she was in company, did they not? Her reputation was safe, if only for this evening, this one night.

Besides, one day she would marry a gentleman who would be undoubtedly dull and boring, someone safe, someone her parents and all of Society approved of. He would not kiss her as Orlando did, touch her like Orlando did, make her feel…well, all this warmth and heat and desire and longing.

Just once, Sophia wanted to know what it would be like to be made love to by a gentleman who knew what he was doing.

Surely there was not anyone in the *ton* who knew what they were doing quite as well as Orlando Dunbar.

"Come on, Sophia Fitzroy, youngest sister of six, who wished for a scandalous romance," Orlando said, letting go of her suddenly and taking three steps up the stairs. "This is your chance. Take it or leave it."

Sophia swallowed. This was her chance. Her chance to be loved by a man she truly cared for. A chance to experience passion perhaps for the first and only time.

Her legs felt shaky as she stepped up alongside him on the stairs.

"Oh, Sophia, you do impress me," said Orlando with a grin. "But I always knew you would."

He took her hand in his, and Sophia could feel his excited pulse throb by his wrist, knew he was just as warm for her as she was for him. The knowledge comforted her in a way she had not expected. She desired him, yes…but he desired *her*.

They had reached the top of the staircase before she realized it, and Orlando stepped forward, pulling her along with him, and opened the door straight ahead of them.

"Welcome," he said, "to my pleasure room."

Sophia's jaw dropped. Now *this* was precisely what she had expected.

The bedchamber was huge—though perhaps that was just

the perception it gave, so filled was it with things designed for human pleasure.

The bed itself was large, a four-poster with red, silken sheets. Candles were abundant, perhaps one hundred of them, on console tables, on the floor, on the mantlepiece... There was a chaise longue, two armchairs, and a chair that looked strangely designed for sitting in, but could be used for...

Sophia's cheeks seared with heat. Oh.

There were feathers, what appeared to be copious ribbons, and by the bed...

"I did promise you would eat," said Orlando, pulling Sophia into the room and closing the door. "Did I not?"

Sophia swallowed. She had not expected this—and yet she had. But seeing it all before her, seeing just what he wished to do...

Beside the bed were several baskets. Just from one glance, Sophia could see cream, honey, strawberries, liquid chocolate...

It was all too much. Yet seeing it all before her, Orlando beside her, knowing what he could do with just a kiss—Sophia shivered. She wanted it. All of it. Wanted to know what it was to be loved, to be touched, to be adored.

And now she could. With Orlando. A man who made her shiver with anticipation just by his mere presence.

"Sophia?"

She turned to him and saw with surprise there was a rather concerned look on his face.

Concern? Orlando?

"I never hide what I want," said Orlando softly. He had let go of her hand. "You know me, Sophia, perhaps better than anyone. I have hid nothing from you, and this is what I want."

What he wanted? "Which is?"

"You."

Sophia took a deep breath. He wanted her. Well, she wanted him, even if she could not quite understand where it would lead. Strawberries and cream?

But she could never leave this room now without knowing, that was certain. Whatever happened, she would have no regrets, for she would share it with a gentleman who knew precisely how to give pleasure.

"Tell me what to do."

Orlando groaned and pulled her into his arms, bestowing a ravishing kiss on her lips before saying breathlessly, "I knew it, the moment I saw you. I knew I would have you—damn, Sophia, you are going to… Right. First things first."

He released her, and Sophia almost moaned at the loss of him. She felt bereft, empty when he was not touching her—but her moan soon transformed into a gasp as she watched Orlando tear off his jacket, waistcoat, cravat, shirt.

Sophia swallowed. He was…well, *beautiful* was not a word typically ascribed to men, but she could think of no better description. A strong, broad chest, dark, wiry hair that spread across then trailed down…

Down to somewhere she could not think of, not just yet.

"Wh-what are you doing?" she managed to ask.

Orlando grinned. "Well, I thought it polite to be the first to remove one's clothes."

The first. Sophia's heart thundered in her chest, but she was surprised to find there was no dread within her. No, this felt…natural. Right. As though all her life had been leading up to this moment, and now she was here, it was the most ordinary thing in the world.

"Well, in that case," she found herself saying, "far be it from me to abandon you."

Orlando stared in amazement as Sophia's fingers gently quested to the buttons on the side of her gown. "S-Sophia?"

She had never heard him like that before, hesitant and eager all at the same time. His eyes did not leave her, hungry yet restrained, as Sophia gently lowered the unbuttoned gown over her under-shift and down to the floor. Without a second thought, she dropped the gown.

Orlando groaned. "Damn, I thought it would take all night to get you out of that!"

"Who said that women do not have…needs? Urges?" whispered Sophia, not sure where this boldness was coming from, but knowing she had to speak now, or never again. "I would have thought you the expert on knowing that a woman wants to be pleased."

She watched as Orlando licked his lips, apparently out of words, and a rush of power and delight soared through her. She was not the only one hungry in this room.

"And…and the rest?"

Sophia almost laughed at the desperation in his voice. Oh, he wanted her—and that knowledge, that Orlando craved her just as she craved him, gave her confidence she had never known before.

"First you," she said lightly.

Orlando moaned, desperately pulling at his boots and breeches, all while trying not to look away from her. He almost fell in his eagerness, and Sophia laughed. His cheeks flushed as he straightened up, entirely naked.

Sophia stared. Well, this was no place to feel shy about her curiosity, was it?

There he stood, all of him. Orlando's erect manhood was twitching, and Sophia felt a pooling rush of heat within her, settling between her legs.

There it was, that part of him that could please, and pleasure.

"Sophia?"

Sophia looked at Orlando's face to see him gazing at her beseechingly.

"Please," he whispered.

There was no going back from this. Slowly, Sophia untied her under-shift and her stays, and allowed both to fall to the floor.

She was entirely naked, and before a gentleman—a gentleman to whom she was not married, nor even engaged. She was ruined. Quite heartly ruined.

Sophia was surprised to find she did not mind a bit.

"You are so beautiful."

A flush tinged her cheeks. "Nothing to your three French hens, I am sure."

"Yes, nothing," breathed Orlando, but before she had a chance to be offended, he continued, "You are far superior. Now, lie on the bed."

Sophia glanced at the bed. It was only a few steps away, but it felt like an eternity before she could feel the soft silk sheets on her back, her head resting on a pillow.

Heart racing, she looked up. "Orlando?"

Touch me, she wanted to say. *Kiss me. Love me.*

Were those the right words, the right things to ask? She did not know, could not know what he expected of her. All she knew was that she wanted all he could give, whatever it was, and would take her fill until she could take no more.

Orlando was standing by the bed, looking hungrily down at her body. "Stay very still."

Sophia nodded, not trusting her voice, then gasped as Orlando picked up a handful of sliced strawberries and started placing them inexplicably on her body.

"Orlando, what—"

"Trust me," he said.

Sophia swallowed and tried not to think how strange she must look—but there was something in the way the fruit touched her, nestled between her breasts, lay on her legs, that felt most…unusual.

Orlando moaned as he clambered onto the bed. "Oh, Sophia…I could eat you all up."

Sophia gasped, unable to help herself, as Orlando bowed his head and gently lifted a strawberry on her thigh off with his lips. The gentle graze of his mouth on her skin sparked tingles across her body, tingles that spread to every inch of her.

"Orlando…"

He kissed her, and Sophia gasped in his mouth, tasting the strawberry and his desire mingling into one flavor that was most delightful.

"Again," she said.

Orlando growled as he lowered his head to her stomach, and Sophia twisted in pleasure at the strange sensation.

Was this what everyone else shared, she wondered wildly as he nibbled at a strawberry lying just below her breast? Was this heady, delicious confusion of scents and smells and tastes and touches what all women were gifted—or was this just Orlando?

There was only one strawberry left now, nestling by her collarbone and her neck. Sophia moaned slightly as Orlando took it between his teeth, grazing her skin.

"Orlando, I want—"

"Yes?" he said, kissing her neck this time and causing shoots of pleasure to rush through her body, his chest pressed up against hers.

Sophia blinked, trying to think, though that was becoming difficult. "I want more."

"Damn, woman, of course you do. Stay still."

She would have remained precisely still, of course, if it meant more pleasure like that—but Sophia could not help but gasp as Orlando drizzled honey across her breasts and thighs.

"Orlando!"

"Trust me," he said, placing the pot of honey down beside the bed. "You'll like this even more."

Surely he was not going to—

"Orlando!"

This time her cry was more a moan as Orlando licked around her nipple, and the stickiness and the sweetness were more pleasurable than anything Sophia had ever experienced.

"You like that?" he murmured as he licked the honey from the top of her breasts then moved to the other nipple, swirling his tongue around it.

Sophia grabbed handfuls of the silk sheet, hardly able to breathe. Was this what all ladies discovered? No wonder so many people lost their reputations—why would you not wish to experience this every day, every night?

"Sophia?"

"Lick me," she whispered, hardly daring to speak such words. "Taste me."

Orlando lowered his head to lick her stomach, then her hips as honey dribbled down onto the sheets, then he kissed her thighs.

Sophia arched her back as the heady sensation of Orlando's tongue on her inner thigh pooled even more heat between her legs. Oh, this was heavenly, this was glorious—surely nothing could surpass this?

"You taste wonderful," murmured Orlando from her thighs.

Sophia managed to laugh. "You mean the honey tastes wonderful."

"Oh, Sophia, Sophia, what have you done," he said, for some reason parting her knees even further and nestling himself between her legs. "Now you've made me do it."

"Do wh—Orlando!"

If Sophia could have jerked upright, she would have, but Orlando's hands were firmly grasping her hips, keeping her steady as his tongue darted into her secret place and tasted of her very inner sweetness.

Stars appeared in Sophia's eyes as she fell back, moaning, twisting, arching her back and releasing the silk sheets only to grab Orlando's hair and pull him closer.

Oh, this was everything, more than she could bear—this was pleasure as she had never known, and her whole body was sparking, scalding, and Orlando's tongue seemed to know just how she wanted to be kissed, possessed, and it was building to something she could not understand but had to know, and—

"Orlando!" Sophia cried as her body exploded, ecstasy tearing at her very limbs.

Violent shaking overtook her as Orlando unrelentingly kissed her, licked her, teased her, and only when she fell back, utterly exhausted, did he lift his mouth from her.

"I was right," came his voice as Sophia wondered when her vision would come back. Stars still circled ahead. "You do taste wonderful."

She blinked several times as Orlando came back into view. "You…you…"

"Now the question is," he said with a wide grin, moving into her eager embrace, "do you want more?"

Sophia stared. "More? Oh!"

His response was immediate and caused ripples of pleasure to swiftly return to her body. His manhood was in her, and she was so warm and wet and pleasure-worn that he slid right into her without any resistance.

"More?" Sophia breathed, looking deep into Orlando's eyes. "There's more?"

"Oh, so much more, more I wish to show you," he said eagerly as he almost entirely withdrew himself then thrust back into her. Sophia moaned as he continued, "More than you could ever imagine. More than we could experience in merely one night together."

Sophia tried to speak, but it was impossible to, not while he was thrusting into her, his mouth alternating between whispering precisely what he wanted to do to her next and kissing her neck, her breasts, and she gave herself up to the pleasure that was building and building, until she could not help herself.

"Give it to me! All of it! Oh, Orlando!"

The cresting ecstasy she now knew rose again, and Sophia quivered, shaking as the pleasure rushed through her, and Orlando seemed to join her, crying out her name and collapsing into her waiting arms.

The two of them lay together in silence, save for panting breaths.

Sophia swallowed. Well, she had done it. She had made love. There was no going back from this—and she was rather delighted to find she had no wish to.

"Orlando?"

"Mmm?" He looked up, eyes hazy, a pleasant sort of tiredness around his eyes.

Sophia grinned wickedly. "I think you mentioned more?"

CHAPTER NINE

WHEN SOPHIA AWOKE, it was into darkness and red silk sheets.

"Give it to me! All of it! Oh, Orlando!"

A smile flickered across her face as the memories from the previous evening started to seep into her mind.

The strange arrival of Orlando and his ridiculous speech before her family about officially wishing to court her.

"After a pleasant walk with your daughter at Hyde Park, she pointed out to me how very remiss I had been in not requesting your permission to court her. And so, of course, once I had completed a little...business, I decided to rectify that mistake immediately."

The way he had spoken to her father... *Lied* to her father, though of course she had not known that at the time.

"Well, I may have lied, just a little, to your father..."

The invitation she had received to come upstairs at Orlando's home, and taste of the pleasures that he wished to share with her...

"I was right. You do taste wonderful."

Sophia shivered slightly, though she was perfectly warm in the large bed. Oh, he had offered her pleasure, and she had taken every mote she could. Wild memories soared into her mind, mingling and tangling, just as their naked bodies had mere hours ago.

Food and pleasure. Who would have known the two were such a marvelous mixture?

Sophia's smile broadened. Right at the end of the night, when she had admitted she could take no more and Orlando admitted he was not sure he had anything more to give, he had ordered a bath—thankfully, she had been able to hide when the servant brought up copious kettles of hot water—and they washed each other, removing the honey, the cream, the strawberries, the chocolate, and the evidence of just how much Orlando had enjoyed her...

And they had fallen asleep.

Sophia glanced over at the gentleman beside her. Orlando was still sleeping, an innocent smile entirely unlike him on his face as he dreamed, one hand tucked behind his head.

Oh, this man. This darling man. This man who knew precisely how to touch her, hold her, tease her, then push her over the crest of something inside her that unraveled pleasure she had never known.

A man who had been patient, and astonished at the way Sophia took then demanded pleasure. He was someone special, Sophia knew. Far more special than anyone she had ever met.

The question was...what was she going to do now?

Sophia looked around the room. From what she could see, though it was still dark, there was no clock. There was no knowing what time it was, but regardless of the precise hour, her family would certainly be expecting her back.

A little tendril of concern encircled her heart. Her sister Esther had gone missing once for a night, and a great deal of upset had been felt in the family. She herself had cried, at least twice, at the thought that something awful had happened to her.

Esther had turned up, of course, on the arm of the Duke of Kendal with a marriage proposal.

Sophia smiled wryly to herself in the dark. She was not so foolish as to expect a repeat of such a thing. She did not need to ask to know Orlando had no intention of matrimony.

But if they could keep this affair secret…why, there was no reason why she could not visit again. And again.

"I cannot stop kissing other ladies because…because…I am not kissing any other ladies."

Sophia sighed happily. She was not the first, and a small part of her was certain she would not be the last.

But she had shared with him something incredibly special—and more, he seemed to enjoy it just as much. Perhaps more. Sophia was not entirely sure what to expect of a man during lovemaking, but did they cry out so swiftly and so often?

"You are thinking about me."

Sophia started, then smiled at the slowly waking gentleman beside her. "Of course I am. I am thinking what a fool I have lying here beside me, when he could be making love to me."

Orlando chuckled dryly. "I am almost embarrassed to admit I do not think I could help you in that regard—at least, not with my manhood. My fingers and tongue are entirely at your disposal, but you have exhausted me, for which I believe you should be given a medal. No one else, at least, has managed it."

A spark of delight shot through Sophia's body, and she impulsively moved into Orlando's arms. "I think that is the nicest thing anyone has ever said to me."

He laughed at that. "Dear God, what a miserable life you've led! Well, I hope I have managed to bring a little joy to it—did I? Last night? You truly enjoyed what we shared?"

If Sophia was not entirely mistaken, there was a flutter of genuine concern in Orlando's voice. Did he truly not know?

"I did," she said softly, pulling his arms around her and glorying in the sensation of his skin on hers, her breasts pressed up against his chest. "Now be quiet and hold me."

Orlando breathed out heavily; Sophia heard it and felt it, felt the movement within him, the gentle settling, the relaxing of all muscles, his hands tight around her.

How long they lay there, she did not know. In a way, this was far more intimate than what they had shared the evening before, though she was not entirely sure how she would explain that to anyone.

If, of course, she was going to explain this to anyone.

"Sophia."

"Mmm?" Sophia's eyes had drifted shut, and she saw no reason to open them now. All she wanted to do was feel—feel his warmth, his comfort, his strength.

"I...I have never done this before."

Her eyes snapped open, and she pushed herself up to look into Orlando's green eyes. "Liar."

"I am not lying!" he protested.

Sophia raised an eyebrow. "Do not even attempt to tell me you were an innocent before last night, for I will not believe you."

A wry grin swept across Orlando's face. "Well. Not that, certainly. But this, I mean. Cuddling. I have never done such a thing with any woman before."

Sophia could hardly believe what she was hearing. The great Orlando Dunbar, the viscount who appeared to have done everything with a woman it was physically possible to do—he had promised there was more he could show her—had never...cuddled?

A warmth quite different from the heat of desire rushed through her. "Truly?"

Orlando nodded, his smile sheepish. "I...well, I am glad I am sharing it with you."

Sophia kissed him swiftly on the lips then returned to his arms, clutching him tightly. This was wonderful—a real connection, far deeper than she had expected. Who else had let the Viscount Dunbar slip through their fingers? She certainly never would.

Perhaps an hour passed—Sophia was not entirely sure; she had slipped into a cozy doze—before she was suddenly aware of movement. A lack of him.

"Orlando," she said, opening her eyes and reaching for him as he rose from the bed.

"I am not going too far," he said with a comforting smile. "I feel the need for another bath. Do not worry yourself; I will use the chamber just off here. You stay in bed. Relax. Make yourself at home."

Sophia watched appreciatively as the naked Orlando stepped across the room lazily, evidently unashamed by his nudity, and closed the door to the little chamber where they had bathed but hours ago.

Sighing happily, she fell back onto the bed.

Orlando Dunbar. What a man. What an experience!

She could never have predicted, this time yesterday, that she would have permitted herself to be ravished, wholly and utterly, by a man such as him. But here she was, lying in the viscount's bed, just ready and waiting for a scandal.

Something twisted around her heart, something akin to fear, but not quite. Of course, she could never permit her parents to know such a thing had occurred—the very idea! Even her sisters could never know.

Strawberries, honey, fruit, the thing he did with his tongue inside her...

No, those were secrets she would keep to herself.

How she was going to explain her overnight absence to her parents, however, was another matter. Perhaps she should send a note, explaining that the carriage had been unable to return her— that she had stayed at a friend of Orlando's?

Sophia swallowed. No, she could not lie. Even to her parents, even to avoid such terrible scandal as this would be if the truth was ever discovered, she could not downright lie to them.

Less information was surely better. A short note saying she had stayed overnight and was quite well, and would be home later.

That was all true, wasn't it? Sophia brought her knees to her chest and tried not to smile. Yes, it was all true, though it would leave out some of the juiciest details.

Well, she would have to find a servant to write and take the note—and that meant descending the stairs. What had Orlando said?

"Relax. Make yourself at home."

Sophia rose from the bed and swiftly found a gentleman's bathrobe to cover her nakedness, which felt far wilder now it was morning.

The door onto the landing opened softly, and there was no one about that she could see. Heart racing, as it felt rather rebellious to be traipsing around someone's home wearing nothing but a bathrobe, Sophia stepped onto the landing, then hesitantly down the stairs.

"Ah, good morning, miss."

Sophia swallowed. A servant who had to be a butler was in the hallway, examining the post that had been left on a table. He had not even turned around to look at her, but must have heard her on the stairs.

"G-good morning," she managed.

The servant turned and bowed, quite matter-of-factly, as though he frequently met half-naked women on the stairs.

Which, Sophia reminded herself darkly, he probably did.

"Breakfast?" he asked smoothly.

"Erm...yes," said Sophia, as though that was precisely her purpose for coming downstairs. "Thank you. And some notepaper, if you please, and a servant to run a message to my...to a certain address."

If the servant thought her request odd, it did not show on his face.

He bowed again. "Of course, right away. I apologize now for the lack of honey available for the breakfast table. I appear to be quite bereft of it."

Heat flared in Sophia's face, and she concentrated on descending the last few steps rather than reply.

Before she could say any more, the doorbell rang and the butler turned to the door. "Do excuse me, miss."

Sophia would have much preferred to have the time to slip into the drawing room rather than be found in the Viscount Dunbar's hall, entirely naked but for a gentleman's bathrobe, but there was no time. The butler opened the door before she could say anything, revealing a stunningly beautiful woman in the most splendid gown Sophia had ever seen.

"Hullo, Wright," she said good-naturedly.

The butler bowed. "Miss Smith."

Sophia stared as the woman stepped inside without waiting for an invitation, nor offering an explanation. Dear God, if she was to be recognized...

"Ah, another one of his French hens," said Miss Smith with a laugh. "I should have guessed his lordship would not be alone."

Shame and rage flooded through Sophia as she stared at the woman, who lazily dropped her reticule on a console table and passed her pelisse to the butler.

"Because I am not kissing any other ladies."

He had lied, then. Why had she not expected him to lie? Everyone had told her that Orlando Dunbar was a rake of the first order and would certainly not hesitate to bed as many ladies as he could manage.

Why had she believed him? Trusted him, accepted his word without question that she was the only object of his affections?

"After a pleasant walk with your daughter at Hyde Park, she pointed out to me how very remiss I had been in not requesting your permission to court her. And so, of course, once I had completed a little...business, I decided to rectify that mistake immediately."

He had turned up at her family home and made such a declaration before them all, Sophia thought bitterly. Did he think they were all fools—that they would forget he had done such a thing?

"Where is he, then?" asked Miss Smith with a grin. "He's expecting me, but I dare say you ran him dry last night. You're not one of the French hens I've met before. New?"

Sophia stared at the woman in disbelief. Oh, this was worse than she could ever have expected, worse than she could have dreamed.

He had already arranged for her to be here. *He's expecting me.* Had Orlando simply forgotten his next conquest was arranged so closely, or did he not care?

Did he think her so desperate, so easy to manipulate, that he could do and say whatever he wanted, even inviting his next paramour to his home before she had the opportunity to escape the indignity of being found here?

"N-no," she managed to stammer, hardly aware of why she was bothering to answer the woman but feeling as though she could not merely stand here saying nothing. "No, I am not one of his French hens."

Miss Smith glanced at her. "Oh, English, then. You're pretty, I must say, but not his usual type. Not his type at all."

Misery poured through Sophia's veins, and she turned without a word, rushing as quickly as she could up the stairs. When she burst into the bedchamber, Orlando was not there.

It took her three minutes to get into her gown. Ignoring her stays and under-shift completely, Sophia managed to frantically button enough that the gown would stay on, and that was sufficient.

She had been such a fool. Marriage had not been offered, and she had not expected it—she was not that idiotic, surely.

But Orlando had told her he was not courting anyone else, not kissing anyone else, and that had been a lie—the woman downstairs was more than enough proof of that.

"You're pretty, I must say, but not his usual type. Not his type at all."

Of course she wasn't, Sophia told herself as she looked hurriedly around the room for her shoes, desperate to escape there before Orlando appeared from his bath. She was not Orlando's type, but she had proven herself to be a challenge.

"You do not think that your future wife might…might be upset that you have bedded so many people?"

"Why? Are you applying for the position?"

"Absolutely not."

And he just *had* to overcome a challenge. Now that he had, that would be it. She would never hear from him again, and quite frankly, Sophia thought wretchedly, she had no wish to.

She never wanted to see Orlando Dunbar, viscount, ever again.

After slipping on her shoes and not giving another look at the room where she had discovered and been shown such pleasure, Sophia rushed out of the room and down the stairs.

The woman was gone, though Sophia thought she could still hear her voice in the drawing room. It did not matter. Sophia grasped the door handle wildly and wrenched the door open, not even bothering to close it as she stepped along the path and onto the pavement.

She was leaving and never coming back.

CHAPTER TEN

IT WAS DIFFICULT to see when one's eyes were blinded by tears.

Sophia had never known that, had never discovered it, but she knew now. Thankfully the sun was only halfway risen and the London streets were almost empty as she strode down the pavement, tears prickling her eyes and heart thumping, desperate to put as much distance between herself and the man who had lied to her, tricked her, made her think there was at least some connection between them, as possible.

But it was all false.

"You're pretty, I must say, but not his usual type. Not his type at all."

Sophia's jaw clenched as she turned a corner wildly, not knowing where she was going—or really, where in London she was—but knowing she had to move.

French hen indeed! As though she had offered herself to Orlando in that way, expecting to be…well, a courtesan! A mistress!

What precisely she had thought they would become to each other, Sophia was not entirely sure. She had not thought, had she? Just felt. Just wanted to feel, wanted to know what it was to be felt by Orlando.

And that had been her mistake.

If she had not been so determined to have a scandalous romance, she would never have managed to get herself into this fix.

It was ridiculous!

Sophia tried not to meet the gazes of the few people who were out and about this early in the week leading up to Christmas. She was certain she would see disdain—shock, even—at the sight of a woman like her, unpinned hair flowing down her back in a gown barely buttoned.

Almost respectable.

Keeping her head down and trying not to think about the situation she had left behind, Sophia tried to put her mind to work at figuring out precisely where in London she was—but it was impossible.

Images of wondrous delight from mere hours ago soared into her mind. Orlando eating strawberries from her chest, licking honey from her breasts and thighs, eating her just as hungrily as he had eaten the cream—

"Sophia!"

She was imagining it, Sophia was sure. It was just her mind supplying what she wanted: Orlando calling out her name, desperate to stop her from leaving him.

She was not so foolish as to believe her own ears. It could not be true. That man had no desire for her, not beyond her body. The man would not simply run out of his house to—

"Sophia!"

Sophia turned, heart racing, and saw to her absolute astonishment that there was a madman following her down the street dressed in a bathrobe—and a bathrobe only, she could see as a hem flew up—who looked remarkably like Orlando Dunbar.

Stomach tight and chest heaving, Sophia turned back around and increased her pace, though it was starting to become difficult for two reasons. First, because this was almost as fast as she could walk without breaking out into a run, and second, because it was getting more and more difficult to ignore the—

"Sophia!"

She would not stop. Darting down a street and hoping to goodness someone would take pity on her and rescue her from

Orlando's foolishness, Sophia found, to her surprise, a part of her wished him to catch her.

Wished Orlando to grab her hand, twirl her around, pull her into his arms, and kiss away all her confusion, all her apprehension, all her misgivings. To show her, not just tell her, that he cared for her.

Sophia tried to harden her heart as her pulse quickened, desperately attempting to get to the end of the street before Orlando caught up with her. She would not listen; she did not want to hear any of his excuses, was tired of being treated like a fool by him.

"Because I am not kissing any other ladies."

No, the last thing she wished to do was—

"Sophia, stop!"

A hand grabbed her own, and Sophia found herself twirled around, but she managed to wrench herself from Orlando's grip before he pulled her into an embrace. At least, that was what she assumed he would attempt to do. And only a small part of her hoped he would. A very small part.

Panting after such exertion, Sophia glared into the face of the gentleman who had utterly betrayed her. "What?"

"What do you mean, what?" Orlando said, evidently at a loss. "Sophia, you cannot suddenly leave like that and not say anything to me!"

"And you cannot be out here like—like that!" Sophia said, relieved the street was empty as she gestured at Orlando's... It could not be called clothes, as it was barely covering him!

"You cannot just disappear. I forbid it," he said.

Sophia glared. He forbade her, did he? Since when did the great Orlando Dunbar think he could order her about?

Oh, he was very much mistaken if he believed he would overwhelm her! She was not for overwhelming. This was not a gentleman who could order her about!

Certainly not when one of his mistresses had just arrived at the door!

"You cannot tell me what to do," she said, hoping her voice sounded far more certain than she felt. "How dare you!"

"How dare I? How dare you simply abandon me, no note, no message with Wright, nothing!" Orlando was staring at her as though she was utterly out of her wits. "Sophia, after all we have shared, all we… You do not think you owe me that?"

Sophia swelled with outrage. *She*, owe *him*? Oh, he was a scoundrel. Arabella had been right. Sophia should never have permitted herself to give him the time of day after discovering his rakish past.

And now look! She was standing in a freezing December street just a week before Christmas, innocence entirely lost, with a gentleman who did not care about her a whit, standing in a bathrobe!

"Owe you?" she repeated, taking a step forward. Orlando took a hesitant step back. "Owe *you*?"

"You cannot just disappear after I…I've fallen in love with you."

Sophia stared. Those words were all ones she recognized, and they had definitely come out of Orlando's mouth. But they did not make sense. Orlando could not have said… He did not mean that he…

Why would he say such a thing?

Discomfort flickered across her heart, and Sophia tried to speak, but had no idea what to say. What did one say to a cad who'd just admitted his affection for you?

If she could believe a word he said, of course. Sophia attempted to harden her heart, telling herself there was no reason at all she should trust him, the blackguard. Had he not invited her into his home, lying to her father to boot, only to seduce her then cast her aside when another woman came to—to service him?

"I beg your pardon?" she managed to ask.

There was a sort of awkward smile on Orlando's face, but he looked earnest as he said, "I…I have fallen in love with you."

Sophia swallowed. This could not be real—this was a trick.

That, or she had never woken up and was still asleep in that large, delicious, soft bed!

"You're lying," she said without thinking.

Well, it was what any other reasonable woman would think, wasn't it? But Sophia was astonished to see genuine pain flash across Orlando's face at the accusation.

"Why would I lie about that?"

"Why would you mean it?" Sophia asked, words tumbling from her lips. "I mean, for goodness' sake, Orlando, you are the Viscount Dunbar! You bed women—you don't fall in love with them!"

"That was true," Orlando said quietly. "Until last night."

Sophia opened her mouth to speak, hesitated, then closed it again.

No, it was all lies—he merely wished to appease her after the sudden appearance of his other woman. He wished to ensure they could repeat last night, and a rush of desire surged in Sophia as she thought of what they had shared, the pleasure they had exchanged, the way his tongue had...

Sophia pushed aside the thought hurriedly. No, she would not be one of those women who was easily calmed just because a man could kiss like the devil.

"I never meant to fall in love with you, but I could not help it," said Orlando quickly, as though he was being given his opportunity to prove himself. "Damnit, Sophia, what man could help it?"

She laughed dryly. "Plenty have."

"But none of them know you like I do," Orlando said, taking a step forward. Sophia did not move, could not move, only think. "Sophia, you are the most beautiful—"

"Oh, I do not want to hear any of your well-practiced compliments," she said darkly, turning away.

Was the man a fool? Could he not see that she was not to be so easily taken in?

A hand gingerly touched her shoulder, and Sophia allowed

herself, against her better judgment, to be turned around.

There was a strange look on Orlando's face, as though he was in physical pain at the thought she would disbelieve him.

"You are the most beautiful woman I have ever met," he said seriously, "but also the bravest. The boldest. A woman who quite literally took my breath away when I left my house almost naked to run after you because I do not want to lose you."

Sophia swallowed. It was a heady thought indeed, that he had done such a thing because he cared for her…

"You love me?" she said.

Orlando nodded. "It's either that, or I have a serious case of gout, because I ache for you, Sophia. It was agony to leave you to take a bath, but nothing to the pain of discovering you had gone. Sophia—"

"Don't you *Sophia* me," she said. "You are speaking nonsense, Orlando—even you must realize how nonsensical you sound!"

"Does speaking from the heart make one sound like a madman, for if so—"

"Orlando!" Sophia glared, pushed past all endurance.

What was she going to do with this man?

"What about your three French hens?" she shot back at him, and she was half pleased, half saddened to see Orlando blanch. "What about Miss Smith? What about Miss Tilbury, and all the other ladies of the *ton* you service with your lovemaking?"

"You're pretty, I must say, but not his usual type. Not his type at all."

Sophia tried to push aside the memory of that woman. It was not her fault, of course—it was all Orlando's fault. How many others would be appearing throughout the rest of the day for him to take his fill?

"All these women who want you," Sophia said, not sure how she could argue any longer. "All of them beautiful, all of them eager for you to—"

"They may want me, but I want you," Orlando interrupted. He raised a hand, cupping Sophia's cheek gently. She did not turn away. "What do I have to say to you to make you believe me? Sophia, I am well practiced in the art of making love, but falling in love? This is all new to me. I need you. I cannot exist without you. Please. Don't leave me."

Sophia swallowed. His hand was warm against hers, gentle, caring, yet with the delectable promise within of the ability to give such pleasure. Such tenderness.

For that was what it had become, had it not? Their lovemaking had been dark, and delicious, and desperate at first, as he had shown her just what it was to feel agonies of ecstasy. But over time, as the night had continued, had it not become sweet? Tender? Had he not opened himself to her, shown her what he wanted, moaned her name as she caressed him?

"All those other ladies, I...I don't want them anymore," Orlando said. He had stepped closer, Sophia was not entirely sure when, but his chest was grazing hers—his actual chest, as his bathrobe had come slightly untied. "I want you."

And she wanted to believe it. As Sophia looked up into Orlando's green eyes, she saw only honesty and desperation there. He was not lying—at least, she did not think he was lying. There was no malice there, no teasing look.

"I... You..." Sophia cleared her throat, conscious that her hands had somehow placed themselves on Orlando's hips, keeping him close. "You lied to my father."

"I will make it up to him," said Orlando softly, "by marrying his daughter. As he said I could, last night, when I asked him for your hand in marriage."

Sophia stared. "You...what?"

There was a wry smile on his face now, all eagerness and awkwardness. "I had never done such a thing before, you understand, so I am not entirely sure if I gave the right speech, but...well, I spoke from the heart. He seemed to understand."

Her heart leapt. He wanted to marry her. He had already asked her father. Could it be true? "You will regret it."

"I doubt that very much," Orlando said tenderly, a smile

dancing on his lips.

Sophia smiled weakly. Well, this was not what she had expected at all. A scandalous romance indeed, but the three French hens and Miss Tilbury and Miss Smith, and all the other ladies of the *ton*, were going to be disappointed by the news that would soon be announced.

Very soon, if she had anything to do with it.

"This will come back to bite you," Sophia said with a teasing smile, heart quickening and that warmth she knew pooling between her legs. "I am not the easiest person to live with."

"That I can well believe," said Orlando dryly. "But I would rather be annoyed by you than kiss anyone else."

Sophia reached up on her tiptoes and kissed Orlando hard on the mouth. He was hers. She was his. There was no other way around it, no way to untangle them; their hearts were one, just as their bodies had been one last night.

And would be again soon, if that hard throbbing against her hip was any sign…

Orlando broke the kiss and grinned. "I think we are rather making a scene."

Sophia glanced around and saw a gaggle of people pointing at them—well, pointing at Orlando, mainly. Few gentlemen meandered around the streets of London in only a bathrobe, even at Christmas.

"In that case," she said with a grin, "perhaps it is time to return home and…eat."

Orlando's eyes widened. "You minx."

"Far better than your three French hens," Sophia said, slipping her hand in his as they started to walk back to his home.

"Oh, so much better."

About Emily E K Murdoch

If you love falling in love, then you've come to the right place.

I am a historian and writer and have a varied career to date: from examining medieval manuscripts to designing museum exhibitions, to working as a researcher for the BBC to working for the National Trust.

My books range from England 1050 to Texas 1848, and I can't wait for you to fall in love with my heroes and heroines!

Follow me on twitter and instagram @emilyekmurdoch, find me on facebook at facebook.com/theemilyekmurdoch, and read my blog at www.emilyekmurdoch.com.